D1808410

WATER LANE

WATER LANE

Tom Aitken

HODDER AND STOUGHTON
LONDON SYDNEY AUCKLAND TORONTO

British Library Cataloguing in Publication Data
Aitken, Tom
    Water Lane.
    I. Title
    823'.914[F]   PR6051.17

    ISBN 0-340-38560-X

Copyright © Tom Aitken 1986

First published 1986

All rights reserved. No part of this publication may be
reproduced or transmitted, in any form or by any means,
electronic or mechanical, including photocopy, recording,
or any information storage and retrieval system, without
permission in writing from the publishers.

Published by Hodder and Stoughton Children's Books,
a division of Hodder and Stoughton Ltd,
Mill Road, Dunton Green, Sevenoaks, Kent TN13 2YJ

Photoset by Rowland Phototypesetting Ltd,
Bury St Edmunds, Suffolk

Printed in Great Britain by T. J. Press (Padstow) Ltd,
Padstow, Cornwall

For Brian Weeden

How It Started

Billy's head felt as if it was falling off his shoulders. He tried to sit up straight but his neck had gone weak and he couldn't. Something behind his eyes was tumbling round and round like a body falling through space.

He heard a sound a long way away, like a downstairs door opening quietly. He looked towards his own door, but his eyes didn't get that far. All he could see was the pattern on the wallpaper dancing.

He stood up, but felt sick straight away and sat down again. The can he'd been holding in his left hand and the polythene bag from his right fell to the floor.

Then he must have gone to sleep.

When he came to, he found he could sit up. He could also see clearly again, and what he saw was a mess on his boot and on the bedside rug.

He grabbed the can and bag and put them on the bedside table. The glue had set hard on his boot and the rug. He couldn't wipe it off.

He knew what his mum and dad would say if they found out what he'd been doing. The stuff would have to be got off somehow. On tip-toe, he went to the door and opened it. They couldn't be back from the pub yet, because there was no sound in the house and no lights on downstairs. No light under Mandy's door either.

He got a sharp knife from the kitchen and scraped at the rug. Some flaked off fairly easily, but he had to cut away a few bits of wool where it wouldn't budge. He didn't think it would show.

The knife was useless on his boot. It scratched the leather, making it look worse. He'd have to leave it until he thought of a better way.

7

He put the can in a box under his bed and took the knife and polythene bag downstairs. The bag went in the rubbish bin outside, under the last lot of potato peelings. The knife he gave a good clean before putting it back in the drawer. Then he went to bed, and was asleep before his mum and dad got home.

PART ONE

Chapter One

Billy was the first to arrive at the place where they liked to fish. He'd managed to stay out of trouble at school so he wasn't kept in, even though he had Miss Richards for two periods on Thursday afternoon. She made some greasy comment about his behaviour improving. He said 'Yes, miss,' and got away as soon as he could.

Mandy wasn't home from junior school, so he grabbed a can of Pepsi and a bag of crisps, collected his fishing bag from the garden shed and biked off to the river straight away.

Their mum wouldn't let him keep his fishing tackle in the house. She didn't want the place stinking of fish, she said. Mandy reckoned he never caught any, so it couldn't stink, and Billy didn't know whether to say she was a liar – because then he'd have to argue with their mum about the smell – or shut up. Then Mum changed her mind and said it wasn't the smell really, it was the damp, and Billy said he always dried everything off properly. He tried to persuade her his gear wouldn't be safe in the shed, with thieves and burglars and everything. Mandy said no one was going to burgle the shed when they could nick the colour telly from the house and their mum had said he was the last person to talk about thieves. Then she looked funny, as if she wished she hadn't said that, and his gear stayed in the shed and he belted Mandy afterwards when their mum wasn't looking.

It wasn't far from their house to the river. They didn't live on the snobs' side with the hill and the park and all that, but on an estate where the docks used to be, ages ago. It was flat and the streets were all straight lines and the houses were all new. Billy liked it. He didn't like things to be old. Although he fished at Thamesford every time he could, he only ever went into the old bit in the town centre to collect his papers in the morning, even though it was just up Water Lane from where they fished.

When he got to the river, Billy did what he would never have let anyone else do: he rode his bike down the wide steps that took you from the end of the bridge to the tow-path. There was no one on the steps but a fair number of people on the wide bit of the tow-path, because people liked to walk and sit there when there was any sun. It was warm now, with a bit of wind getting up along the river. Billy thought about how that would affect the water and the fish.

He rode along in front of the boatsheds to the bit where they fished, at the bottom of Water Lane. There was a tree in a sort of big concrete tub with seats. Billy sped up and zoomed around it, leaning right over. Then he jumped off and chained the bike to the railings that were supposed to stop you falling into the ramp which ran down into the water from the bottom of the lane, where boats could pull in when the tide was high. It was low now and the ramp was drying out. You could see where the concrete had broken and there was a sharp drop of about a foot. Billy always had a laugh when people brought a boat down Water Lane on their luggage rack or a trailer and unloaded it at the ramp to slide it into the water. If they hadn't been there before and the tide was in someone always fell over and got his trousers wet. Sometimes a lot more than that.

The tide was so low now that you could see patches of riverbed and the current looked almost as if it had stopped. In a while it would flow back upriver and the level would rise about a metre, nearly up to the path. When that happened they'd close the floodgates by the lock just downstream – so that the river and the tide between them wouldn't flood London, Dad said.

Billy unstrapped his fishing bag from the back of his bike and spread his tackle out on the paving stones. He still treated it very carefully, even though it was a year since he'd bought it. He'd earned the money himself from his paper round. Now he was saving up for a Walkman.

He chucked a handful of maggots into the water as ground-bait, then put together the three sections of his hollow glass fibre match rod. When the line was running smoothly, he set the float so that the bait would lie just above the riverbed, and did an underhand cast. It was a good one, with hardly any splash. He sat on the edge of the tow-path watching the float and the posh swing-tip bite indicator his gran had given him.

He thought he'd stay about an hour and a half and be home for his tea at seven. Jake and Sharon would probably come along for a while. Mandy would likely turn up as well to pester him.

Opposite him, someone was on one of the boats by the island, slopping water about the deck from a bucket. The island was covered in willows which had long thin branches like strings with thousands of leaves tied to them, as if they were Christmas decorations someone had gone mad over. There was a line of motor boats moored in front of it, like the line of ducks on his gran's bathroom wall. If he ever had enough money, Billy wanted a boat. It'd be great to be able to go up and down the river under the bridges and through the lock gates, down as far as London, maybe.

The float dipped sharply, then plunged under the water. Billy was taken by surprise and he struck badly. Instead of making a firm upward sweep with the rod, he yanked at it suddenly and the tackle came flying out of the water at him. No fish on it of course. Lucky none of the others had turned up yet or he'd never have heard the end of it. Mandy would have gone on all through tea.

He rebaited the hook, cast again, and chucked in a few more maggots. This time he'd concentrate.

'Hello, Billy.'

The voice was behind him. So was the sound of polished brown leather shoes with metal heel and toe plates. They didn't scrape on the paving stones, they tapped them sharply, like a pony trotting very slowly, because this was the Colonel. He lived by himself in one of the three small houses which were downstream of Water Lane and knew Billy because he was always up and about when Billy came with the paper, not still snoring, like all the other customers.

He was quite a nice old guy, who never told Billy what to do and what not to do. He had a bald head like a brown egg and a little moustache like a worn-out toothbrush that had gone grey.

In the afternoon he usually walked along the river past the bridge to where there were some fields. He'd look at the cows and then go back home. Sometimes, if it was warm, he'd bring a deck chair and sit three or four metres away from Billy and the others, not interfering, just watching. When he didn't have the chair he liked to keep moving, slowly, but if he did stand still, he'd rock backwards and forwards on the middle part of his foot, keeping his balance with his walking stick. Billy couldn't imagine how old he was. He was easily the oldest person Billy knew, because Billy's gran – the only grandparent he had left – was quite young for a grandmother.

'Caught anything?' asked the Colonel.

'Just lost one,' said Billy.

'I say. Jolly bad luck.' He really did talk like that. When Billy told his mum, she said he must be making it up until Mandy said Billy was right, that was how the Colonel talked. It was so unusual for Mandy to agree with Billy that their mum had to believe it.

'Better luck next time, eh?' said the Colonel.

'Hope so,' said Billy. He grinned at the Colonel, who smiled back and wrinkled his eyes. He had false teeth and his gums had started to shrink, he said, which was why he sometimes clicked when he talked.

'I'll be off to have a chat with the cows,' he said. He was half-joking. He thought that was what Billy and the others would think about him, so he said it first. He walked away slowly.

It must be about five o'clock. Maybe Jake and Sharon weren't coming. Jake's aunty was ill, he might have had to go

14

and see her. And Sharon spent a lot of time on homework – far more than Billy ever did.

The tide was coming in and his line and float were drifting slightly upstream. The bits of riverbed he'd been able to see when he arrived were covered now. The water was smooth and shining in the sunlight and the launches and trees opposite him were very clearly reflected just like a photo.

Suddenly the water around his float got ripped up. He shouted and swung round. He knew who it had to be, because it was one of Mandy's favourite ways of annoying him.

She was standing there pretending to look as if she hadn't done anything, but Billy could see wet sand on her fingers.

'Get off,' he shouted, and she giggled. She was dancing around in her jeans and tee-shirt, just out of reach.

She always mucked him about when she arrived. She was all right after that, especially if the others were here, because they had fixed punishments which she'd have to take if she wanted to stay with them.

Sharon had worked out the punishments after one day when Mandy had been really silly. Billy had got so mad that he'd pushed her into the ramp. It had been dry when he'd last looked at it and the worst he'd thought she'd get was muddy feet. He'd forgotten about the tide. They'd had to pull her out.

Luckily, the Colonel had come along, and he'd taken her and Sharon to his house to dry her off. Billy had watched her squelching along the dry tow-path leaving a trail of water, wondering what their mum and dad would say.

It hadn't been too bad, in the end, because Mandy had liked sitting in the Colonel's front room in an old dressing gown, looking at the Colonel's books with Sharon while her soaking shirt and jeans steamed in front of a gas fire. So she hadn't grumbled much when they went home and all Billy got was what his dad called a 'firm warning'.

Next day Sharon told Mandy that if she mucked about she'd have to walk along to the bridge and count up to a hundred before she came back. If she mucked about again, it would be up Water Lane to the top and counting up to two hundred.

Mandy grumbled so much that they sent her along to the bridge straight away.

Anyway, she'd have someone else to pester now, because Jake was wandering down Water Lane. He waved at Billy, then stopped to look in the entrance of one of the old warehouses. There was nothing kept in them now, although one or two had notices warning you to keep out and beware of guard dogs.

Jake was a West Indian whose real name was Jacob. He was always very neat, with a proper crease in his trousers and a tie. He had a megasize grin and was hardly ever upset no matter what happened. Mandy like him as much as Billy did, and would do anything he said.

'Hi,' said Jake when he arrived.

'Hi,' said Billy.

'Jake,' said Mandy, 'Billy's mad because he would have caught a huge fish just now if I hadn't chucked some gravel in the water.'

Jake grabbed her wrist and pretended to force it up behind her back. 'We have ways of making you sorry!' he shouted. Like Billy's, his voice wasn't quite broken, and it sounded sometimes like a girl's and sometimes like a noise echoing out of an empty petrol tin. Sometimes it just squeaked.

Mandy jumped around screaming. Billy reeled in his line. You had to wait for this to be over. There was no way you could stop it happening.

When they got tired of it, Jake and Mandy sat down by Billy and swung their legs against the embankment. Billy checked his bait and cast again. He reckoned there weren't many fish about. He'd just have a laugh with the others and go home.

'Sharon coming?' he asked.

'Nah. She's got to do her French.' Jake and Sharon were in the same class and they went to the same church. They'd always been friends. 'She'll be here Saturday.'

'You not doing it?'

'The French? Done it in the bus on the way home.'

Jake was careful never to do any of his work too well. He

16

was clever and was in a higher class than Billy. He wanted to do O-levels, but reckoned if you worked too hard too soon that was grovelling to the teachers. He saved himself for the exams, he said, and he did usually get quite good marks.

'Where's your gear?' asked Billy. Jake had once been very keen on fishing. That was how he and Billy started meeting here. But lately he'd been less interested. He usually brought his gear at the weekends, but on weekdays he didn't bother.

'Can't stay,' said Jake. 'Got to go home.'

'Are you going to see your aunty?' asked Mandy.

'Sunday,' said Jake.

Something was wrong with her but Jake wouldn't say what. Whatever it was he'd been worried about it for quite a while now.

'What's the matter?' asked Mandy, screwing up her eyes. She was a kid, she couldn't take a hint.

'She's sick,' said Jake.

'I knew that,' said Mandy as if Jake was being stupid. 'I mean what's . . .'

She caught sight of Jake's face and shut up. Billy felt uncomfortable. He glared at Mandy and hoped she wouldn't start again.

No one said anything for a while. The Colonel came back from talking to the cows and pretended he was going to push Mandy into the river with his walking stick. She jumped up and ran away giggling and the Colonel went home.

Jake stood up. 'See ya,' he said.

'I hope she's better soon,' said Mandy.

'Yeah,' said Jake.

'Think I'll pack up,' said Billy, and swung his feet up on to the path.

Jake stopped in his tracks. 'What's that on your boot?' he asked.

Billy blushed. He could feel it spreading all over his face and down his neck under his shirt.

'Nothing,' he said.

17

Jake stared at him. 'It doesn't look like nothing to me,' he said.

Billy looked at his foot. He knew perfectly well what Jake was talking about. That rounded white streak, as if someone had dripped bacon fat out of a frying pan there and it had set.

'It's nothing,' he repeated.

Jake stared at him even harder, as if he knew Billy was lying. Would he say so? And what would Billy do then? He couldn't tell Jake to mind his own business. There were all sorts of people Billy wouldn't worry about lying to. But Jake was different.

'I know what it is,' said Mandy.

Billy's stomach seemed to move inside him. He'd thought she was asleep. She must have come and peeped through the door. Perhaps he'd called out or made some other noise without knowing it. He couldn't remember.

'If that's what I think it is,' said Jake, 'you're a fool.'

'I don't know what you mean,' said Billy. He felt frightened and ashamed that he was lying to Jake, but he couldn't just say 'Yes, Martin gave me a can of glue and I had a go and nearly passed out, and dripped it over things.' He couldn't. Mandy would tell. Things had only just calmed down at home after his trouble with the police.

'He does know,' said Mandy. 'I know he does. Tell him, Jake.'

'That's what started my aunty,' said Jake. 'She's on other stuff now, but that's what started her. And you know what she wants to do?'

Billy shook his head. Jake's voice was going all funny because he was upset, but Billy didn't feel like laughing.

'She wants to die.'

Even Mandy shut up when she heard Jake say that. And Billy felt as if someone had kicked him very hard, very low in the stomach.

He took his rod to pieces and put it carefully into its bag. The other two stood and watched him. No one said anything until the way they were staring at him got on Billy's nerves.

18

'Leave me alone, can't you?' he shouted.

'I've got to go home with you, Mum said,' Mandy told him quickly. Jake just shrugged and turned away. He wasn't grinning. And Billy, as he bent over to finish putting everything into the bag, felt himself crying. He didn't know what would happen now.

Chapter Two

When Billy straightened up again, Jake had gone. Mandy thought Billy was looking at her as if he was trying not to lose his temper. She felt nervous. When she told on him, Billy sometimes hit her. And this time it was more serious than usual.

But Billy didn't say anything – just unchained his bike, tied the fishing bag to it, and walked along the tow-path to the road bridge. Mandy had to walk fast to keep up. She helped him carry the bike up the steps to the road and he gave her a weak grin. She could see he'd been crying, but knew it would be silly to say anything.

They walked across the bridge because the traffic was thick and turned behind the big old house with pointed towers. Billy got on to his bike. Mandy waited. He might ride slowly while she walked, or he might leave her behind altogether and dare her to say anything when she got home.

'Hop on,' he said. He held the bike steady until she was safe, then pushed off.

He rode very fast along this bit of narrow road. He wanted her to think he would smash them straight into the wall at the end. She hung on tight. About four metres from the wall he put the brakes on and came practically to a stop, then did a wobbly left turn into the narrow back alley where cycling was forbidden. It was part of Billy's rules for himself that he didn't take his feet off the pedals when he turned like that, and part of his rules for her that she didn't squeal.

He went fairly slowly in the alleys, ready to jump off if certain people came in sight. There was one old lady who threatened to tell the police. Billy reckoned she wouldn't really, but he didn't want any more trouble so soon after the last lot.

They passed a lot of back gardens and a boat-yard.

'Are you gonna tell our Mum?' He muttered the question in her ear as he went round one of the corners.

'Don't know,' she said.

Billy stopped the bike and got off. They'd come out of the alleys and were on a bit of lawn at the end of a road, only a couple of streets from their house.

'You'd better not,' said Billy. He wasn't looking at her the way he usually did when he said that. He wasn't looking at her at all. That made her feel a bit cheekier than she would have been sometimes.

'Why?'

She knew then there was something worse wrong than usual, because he said nothing for a minute: not ''Cause I'll belt you one afterwards,' or 'I'll spill ink on your schoolbooks,' or any of the things he usually threatened. He put the bike flat on the grass and kicked at the gutter.

'What'd you see last night?'

She wished he hadn't asked that. What she'd seen had frightened her and she'd tried to forget it. She *had* almost, until Jake had asked Billy what the mark was on his boot was and Billy had blushed like that. She wished she'd seen nothing. She liked Billy and hated it when he was in trouble and Mum and Dad were upset and angry with him.

'What'd you see last night?' He gave the gutter an extra hard kick and looked straight at her. 'What'd you see? Can't you hear me asking? Have I gone invisible or something?'

'I wasn't asleep,' she said, and stopped. It was hard to remember exactly and Billy might belt her one if he thought she was lying or anything.

'That's a big help,' he sneered. 'I thought you must be awake, didn't I, or I wouldn't have asked what you saw.

'I bet you didn't see anything at all. You're just talking, you're trying to find out, aren't you? You couldn't tell our Mum anything, 'cause you didn't see anything to tell.'

'I did, I did, I did see,' Billy must believe her. 'I came to see if

21

you'd play cards with me. You were sitting on your bed.'

'Nothing wrong with that,' he said when she stopped again. But he wanted to hear what she'd say next.

'You were sitting on your bed, looking at the door. You had a red tin and a plastic bag and you were staring.'

'At the door?' asked Billy.

She nodded.

'Now I know you're lying.'

'I'm not, Billy, I'm not. You were staring . . .'

'If I was staring at the door, how come I didn't see you? You weren't coming in through the window, were you?'

'No, I wasn't. I was standing in the doorway. And you didn't see me.'

That was why she had been so frightened. It was frightening just remembering.

'How d'ya know I didn't?' Billy asked her that quickly, trying to make it look as if he'd caught her out. 'I might have been mucking about, pretending not to.' He was staring at her again, but it wasn't anything like the stare she'd got from him last night. This was a normal, bullying, Billy sort of stare. Last night it wasn't only her he wasn't seeing. He wasn't seeing anything.

'I talked to you, and you didn't say anything. And something dribbled out of the plastic bag over your hand and on the rug and your boot. Then you stood up and walked around looking . . .' She didn't know the word for what he'd looked like, but it was really weird. 'I thought you were sick,' she said.

'Why didn't you tell Mum and Dad when they came in then?'

'I heard you go down to the kitchen just before then, so I thought you were all right. You looked all right this morning.'

That was true but he looked very worried now.

'You did see me really, didn't you?' she asked.

'Yeah, of course,' said Billy. He was lying, she knew straight away.

'I saw you. I forgot, that's all.'

Sometimes, if Dad was drunk at night, he forgot things he'd said and done. Like once he'd balanced her teddy over the toilet door for a joke and it had fallen on him when he'd gone in there in the night and he'd shouted and carried on about crazy kids.

But Billy couldn't have been drunk, could he? She didn't think he drank anything. He'd always said it was stupid. Mum and Dad would go really mad if they thought Billy'd been drinking. Dad had said . . . That must be why Billy was so scared of them finding out.

'What was in that tin, Billy?' she asked. 'Was it beer?'

'No, silly,' he said.

'Why did Jake say that about his aunty? About her starting on that and being on something else now?' Sharon had told her something about Jake's aunty's illness which she hadn't really understood, but she thought it meant Jake's aunty was taking . . . No. Billy couldn't be. He wouldn't be such a fool.

'Billy. What was in that tin?'

'Shut up,' Billy said. 'None of your business.'

'I'll tell our Mum what I saw.'

He would have to tell her now. He could threaten her as much as he liked, but he knew she'd seen and he knew she could tell if she wanted to.

'You're being kiddish,' he said.

'I'll tell, I'll tell.' She turned it into a little song and dance, the way she used to when she was small.

He picked up his bike. 'You can walk home,' he said.

'Don't care, don't care. I'll tell, I'll tell, I'll tell.'

Dad didn't like her riding on the bar of Billy's bike and she'd have to walk most of the rest anyway.

'I'll tell you if you promise me . . .' said Billy.

'What? What've I got to promise?' She ran across the grass to him. She'd much rather find out what was in the tin without getting him into trouble.

'You're not to say anything to them.'

23

'What if they ask me? Dad'll belt me if he thinks I know and won't tell.'

Billy wrinkled up his face. He was working out what was riskiest. 'All right. If they ask you. But don't you dare . . .'

'I won't.'

'And when I've told you, you can forget all about it, 'cause I'm going to chuck it away. I'll put it in the rubbish bin. You can watch me. That'll be the end of it.'

'All right. It'll be a secret.'

This was exciting. They used to have secrets when Billy was smaller but he said that was kiddish now, and they hadn't had one for ages.

'Yeah,' said Billy. 'Sort of. I'll tell you what it was, we'll wrap it up and chuck it away and we'll both forget all about it.'

'All right, Billy.'

She waited. He still didn't seem to want to tell her.

'What was it?'

He stood the bike up and patted the bar for her to get on.

'Glue, stupid,' he said.

'Glue?' she repeated, and wanted to giggle. Then she thought of Jake's aunty being ill and didn't. But it did sound silly.

Chapter Three

When they got in, their dad was sitting at the table reading the paper.

'You're late,' he said.

'Sorry, Dad.'

'Catch anything?'

'Nah.'

'Bad luck.'

Dad couldn't see anything in fishing but he seemed pleased that Billy liked it. He said it was healthy and that was more than you could say for a lot of the things kids were interested in these days. So, although he was always on at Billy to do more at school – 'you won't get a job without qualifications' – he didn't mind so much if he hadn't done his homework because he'd been fishing as he did if it was because he'd been watching the telly.

'Get yourselves cleaned up. The tea's nearly ready.'

Their mum came in with a tray. It had a big plate of bread and butter and four plates of fish and chips and frozen peas on it. And the big teapot balanced on the edge.

'Just in time,' she said. 'Another five minutes and your dad would have eaten the lot.' She put the tray on the table and came over to them and bent down. Billy and Mandy had to kiss her cheek. 'Put that fishing bag out the back and wash your hands. Quickly.'

Billy and Mandy heard her say, 'Anything on the telly?' as they went out.

'No,' said Dad. He said it in a way that meant tonight was one of the nights when they had to talk to each other and 'be a family'. But, fish and chips, that was all right.

Billy rushed out to the shed and dumped his bag, promising himself he'd clean his tackle properly tomorrow. On his way back to the table he stopped at the kitchen sink and let some water run on his fingers. The others were sitting waiting. Mandy already had a chip in her mouth.

It was all nice and hot and nobody said anything for a while. Dad didn't think to ask them what they'd done at school that day.

'Anything in the paper?' Mum asked.

Dad grunted through a mouthful of chips. 'Just the usual,' he said when he'd swallowed them. 'Prices going up. Vandalism. Another horrible murder.'

'Oh dear,' said Mum, 'isn't it awful? There's never any good news, is there?'

'They reckon a lot of top athletes are taking drugs. You can't stop it, they say, unless you get a quack to check them all out before every race.'

Mum made a clucking sound with her tongue and got on with her fish and chips.

Billy couldn't see why his dad bought the newspaper. It always seemed to make him grumpy. But he said you had to know what was happening in the world and tried to make Billy read it as well. Mandy read the paper more than he did.

He swallowed half a cup of tea at a gulp and stayed out of trouble by going into the kitchen to top up the pot from the kettle. When he came back his mum was asking, 'What was the murder, dear?'

Dad pushed his plate away and filled his cup. He looked at Billy and Mandy as if he didn't want to talk about it in front of them, then said, 'Well, you can both read, I suppose. A teenage boy killed his grandmother. Up in the north somewhere.'

Mum made the sort of moaning sound she always made when she heard something like that. It seemed stupid to Billy. It wasn't anyone they knew, wasn't anything to do with them.

'Why?' she asked. She knew Dad would tell her anyway.

'He was going through her sideboard looking for money when she caught him and told him off. So he killed her, naturally.'

Dad was being sarcastic, as usual, and, as usual, Mum thought he meant it. 'It's not natural at all,' she said. 'I think they should . . .'

'Of course it's not natural,' said Dad, the way he talked when he'd explained something twice and Billy hadn't understood it. 'I mean this young thug didn't think twice about killing his grandmother because she wouldn't let him take what was hers. He happened to need the money, or he wouldn't have killed her, would he?'

'What did he need it for?' Mum asked. It was as if she was trying to find a good reason for what the boy had done, something that would make it seem less awful to her.

Dad said nothing until he knew they were all looking at him. He always liked to make what he said exciting, even if it was really dead boring. Mum seemed to like it, but it made Billy really angry sometimes, especially when he could see Dad thought he was stupid for not knowing before he was told.

'What for? To buy glue, of course. To sniff.'

Mandy went red in the face and looked at Billy. Then she looked away and ate some chips in a hurry. Billy tried to kick her under the table, but missed. The table shook. If Dad hadn't been so busy making a good story out of what he was saying, he would have noticed. When Mum was oohing and aahing the way Dad wanted, he turned to Billy.

'Let that be a warning,' he said.

For a minute Billy felt as if someone had slogged him over the back of the neck with a cricket bat or something. He didn't dare look at Mandy, let alone at Dad or Mum. He mumbled something into his tea. He saw Mandy's hand reach out and take another slice of bread and stuff it into her mouth.

'Everyone finished?' asked Mum, as if nothing had happened.

'Not quite,' said Dad, looking at Mandy. 'Don't gobble, girl. But you can get on with the washing up. You help, Billy.'

'All right.' Billy stood up and collected the fish and chip plates. He'd sussed it out. It'd just been one of the warnings

Dad chucked at him, and even at Mandy, every now and then, because of something he'd read. 'Don't gamble good money on horses', (what was bad money, Billy wanted to know) or 'Don't get into a car with a strange man'.

He took the plates into the kitchen and dumped them in the sink. He ran the hot tap and squirted in some detergent – too much, Mum would say when she saw – and sloshed the water about so that the bubbles came over the edge of the sink. Then Mandy came in, carrying the tray with everything else except the teapot on it. Mum brought that in, to be safe. She was going to stay, but Mandy said, 'You sit down, Mum, we'll do them.'

Mum came up behind her and Billy and kissed them both. She snuggled Billy's neck. Her hair tickled. 'That's lovely, my darlings,' she said. 'Thank you.'

She went back into the other room. There was some mumbling and a click and they heard the sound of the telly. There were two voices shouting at each other, then all the people in the studio laughed. Mum too. Not Dad. He was probably grumping into his paper again.

'You're not going to do it any more, are you, Billy?'

'What?'

'The glue, stupid.'

'Sh! Stupid yourself. Shut up, can't you?'

'They can't hear. You're going to stop, aren't you?'

'Course. I told you. I'll wrap it up and chuck it away.'

'We could do it when we've finished these.'

'If you like.'

'Fancy killing his gran.'

'I wouldn't do that.'

'You mightn't know.'

Billy shut up and got on with the dishes. He didn't want to talk about it. It had felt good, sniffing the stuff, as if he was floating around near the ceiling and everything was all right. At first. The way the pattern on the wallpaper had moved wasn't so good, though, and it really bothered him that he couldn't remember seeing Mandy come in. He must have sniffed too much. He'd chuck it away. He didn't need it the way some people did.

'Where'd you get it?'

That was the trouble about Mandy knowing. She'd keep it a secret but she'd want to know everything. And he'd have to tell her if he wanted her not to tell.

'Martin gave it to me.'

'It was Martin got you in trouble before.'

He wanted to say that was nothing to do with it, but she was right. Martin had told him there was an easy way of picking up bags of sweets in Woolworth's and he'd tried it for a laugh. It seemed to work at first. They'd got outside and about twenty yards away before someone shouted after them and Martin started to run. People grabbed them and hauled them back into the shop while the police were called. They'd given him a great lecture about the right way to start in life, then they'd put him in a panda car and brought him home. Mum had cried all night and Dad had belted him. He'd made Mandy watch.

Billy'd promised to have less to do with Martin, and for a while he did. He only saw him at school anyway, never after school or at weekends. But, yesterday, Martin had suddenly shoved the can into Billy's bag just before registration and told him to keep it out of sight. In registration someone had come and taken Martin off to see the Headmaster. Later they'd heard he was suspended for the rest of the week.

So last night when Mum and Dad went down the pub and he thought Mandy was asleep, he'd got a plastic bag and had a sniff. He'd seen people doing it in the park, so he knew how.

Now that he'd done it, he was almost glad Mandy knew. It would make it easier not to do it again.

They finished the dishes without talking any more. Dad thanked them, from behind the paper, for helping Mum, and said something about homework. Mum smiled at them a lot.

They went upstairs and Billy let Mandy come into his room. He pushed the door shut, then got the glue out of a box of junk he had under the bed.

'Get an old newspaper,' he told Mandy.

She went down to the cupboard under the stairs and he heard her say something about a project for school when they asked her what she was doing.

He made sure the top was tight on the can and wrapped it carefully.

'Will it be all right in the bin?' Mandy asked. 'They might find it.'

'It gets emptied tomorrow.'

She nodded. Then she said, 'I'll put it in the bin now,' and grabbed it and ran downstairs. He sat still, listening to the noise of the front door, and Mum's voice, and Mandy saying she'd found an apple core in her schoolbag.

Mandy came back. 'I wanted to make sure,' she said.

Billy shrugged. 'Forget it,' he said.

Chapter Four

'Brian, has someone been in here? I don't remember that pile of sacking.'

Brian Watson turned back up Water Lane to where Marcia was standing at the entrance to a derelict warehouse. It belonged to their neighbour, Cyril, who was away, and they kept an eye on it for him. He looked through the padlocked wire-mesh gates.

'It's all right,' he said. 'I put it there when I checked the rat traps yesterday. Hullo, Colonel.'

Their other neighbour was tottering down the lane, wrinkling his moustache at them. He waved an evening newspaper as an explanation of what he'd been doing. Normally he was terribly upright and military, but he always found the cobbles in the lane a bit tricky. They walked with him down the lane and along the tow-path.

When they got in, Marcia grilled a couple of steaks and made a salad. After they'd finished eating and loaded the dishes into the washer, she put on a record of the Sacred Mushrooms and made herself a smoke from the materials she kept in a large stone jar marked 'Sugar'. That and the high-pitched drone of the music made her just woozy enough to relax. On the tow-path outside, groups of people wandered past laughing and chattering. The last of the pleasure boats chuntered downstream towards London. People danced on the cabin deck, and the sound of their amplified music momentarily interrupted hers. She lay face down across the huge purple cushion on the floor.

Brian was fussing at the desk in the corner between the fireplace and the windows, taking papers out of folders, muttering at them and putting them back again.

'Aren't you smoking?'

31

'Not yet. I've got to sort out these figures for John.'

'Are they urgent?'

'He wants them phoned through tomorrow and they've got to be just so. You know what he's like. If they don't suit him he won't authorise Hugh to collect the next consignment on Thursday. He's the boss, after all.'

'I want us to be independent of him.' Marcia had never liked the fact that they had had money from John, a man they hardly knew, to start their second business.

'One day, maybe.' Brian sat, quiet, and concentrated for ten minutes or so. The display of his calculator glowed now and again in the thickening dusk. She finished her joint.

'Have you remembered,' he asked when he'd finished, 'there's some stuff still to be shifted?'

'I'll move most of it at the rink on Thursday. Then we'll go to Fiona's party afterwards. (They always went somewhere else as well, the nights she was selling. It was a kind of half-alibi.)

'Right,' he said, moving across the room and standing over her. 'I think I'll have one now.'

'I'll make it for you.' She stood up as he sank into the cushion, and drifted through the house like a leaf floating on the river. It was as easy and natural as that. Life was good. She lived with Brian without the hassle of being married to him. They were well off. They ran two businesses, one of which the law didn't object to.

During the day they worked in the boutique. They were a respectable part of life in Thamesford, members of the Retailers' Association and all that bit. They lived on the river, between a retired Colonel and a man who was a very big noise in local affairs when he was at home.

And, at night, they ran their other business, the one the real money came from, to provide all the mod cons in this expensive little cottage, the motor launch moored a couple of hundred yards away, the luxury hotels when they travelled abroad on business.

By itself, their day-time life would have bored her solid. It was the night-time, with its stealthy loadings and unloadings,

32

the passing of small packets in the glare of the skating rink, the sense of undermining their daylight existence, that gave life its kick. Sometimes, when she met the Colonel on the tow-path on a Thursday evening and he looked at the skates looped over her arm and made those gentlemanly old jokes of his, she wanted to grab his arm and say, 'Come on, Colonel, old boy. Get your own skates on. Join me in a trip. You've been in the Far East, haven't you? Opium dens and all that.'

Would he cry 'Rape!' and send for the police? Or would that little moustache of his wrinkle with pleasure, his watery eyes gleam and his walking stick rattle with excitement, those metal-plated toes of his do a quick tap dance?

She grinned and replaced the stone jar. What rubbish. If the Colonel had a secret life, it would be quite different from hers. No two people were ever the same. Let him do his own thing, whatever it was.

She went back to Brian, lit his joint and kissed him. Then she turned the music up. He looked at his watch.

'It's all right,' she said. 'The Colonel won't complain until midnight, and by then I want us to be upstairs.'

'Why wait till then?' asked Brian through the smoke.

'No reason at all.' She drew the curtains and knelt by the cushion. The drummer on the record got very excited as Brian pulled at the zip of her boiler suit.

Life was good.

Chapter Five

Late Friday night when Billy's Dad got in from the pub, he came into Billy's room. He didn't ask if he could, the way he sometimes did. He marched in and sat at the little table where Billy was supposed to do his homework. Luckily, there was a schoolbook open on it.

Billy was lying on the bed listening to his transistor.

Dad had a plastic carrier bag in his hand. He put it on the floor between them. He looked at Billy's feet, at his Marks and Spencer slippers.

'Get your boots out,' he said.

Billy felt sick. He couldn't say he didn't know where they were because Dad could probably see them under the bed from where he was sitting. There could only be one reason Dad wanted to see them. Mandy must have split on him even though she'd promised.

He got off the bed and crouched between Dad and the boots while he pulled them out. He put them so that the streak of glue was away from Dad and sat on the edge of the bed.

Was Dad drunk? If he was and Billy was in trouble, there would be bruises to show in the morning. But he seemed to be sober. Fairly sober anyway. His eyes weren't funny and he didn't sound as if he was trying to stop his teeth falling out.

He picked up the boot with the streak on it and put it on the table. Then he picked up the carrier bag.

Billy knew what would come out of it. An old copy of the *Sun* with the can of glue wrapped in it. Dad put that on the table too, pushing the schoolbook away. It fell on the floor but he took no notice. (Normally he yelled blue murder if Billy was careless with a book, bent its cover or anything.)

34

He smoothed out the *Sun* and sat back, looking from the can to Billy, from Billy to the can.

Billy sat very still. Dad wouldn't suddenly shout, 'What's the meaning of this!' the way some teachers did. He'd talk about it for a while, going round and round the subject like a dog sniffing at a lamp post. Showing how clever he was. Then, when he thought he had Billy where he wanted him, there'd be a shout and Billy would have to duck.

'This morning,' said Dad, 'I emptied the kitchen tidy in time for the rubbish collection. I saw this can in the bin. Funny, I thought, I didn't know anyone in the house used this stuff. I picked it up. Funnier still, I thought. It's half full. I investigated.'

(That was Dad's favourite word. He liked to say 'I investigated,' and make out to himself that he was Kojak or Scotland Yard or something.)

'I investigated,' he said again. 'Then I remembered this mark on your boot. I'd noticed it yesterday morning and wondered what it was. I couldn't investigate then because you were just leaving for school and I didn't want to make you late. From what I hear you're late too often as it is. But now I can look at it close up, I can see it isn't a chalk mark' – he was scratching at it with his finger nail – 'or a scratch, or bird droppings. It's stuck on and it won't come off.'

He put the boot neatly on the floor with the other one and pushed them both back under the bed with his foot. Billy tensed himself to jump.

'So, Billy,' he went on, 'it's you who's been using this glue. I want to know what for.'

Billy had been so sure he was going to get swiped that he couldn't think for a minute.

'What for, Billy?'

'I . . . there's a break in my fishing rod.' It was the first thing that came into his head. 'I tried to mend it.'

Dad shook his head. He looked sad. 'There isn't. I looked at it before I went out. There's no sign of damage and no glue on it either. I checked your bike as well.

35

'But even if you had been using it to mend something, Billy, why throw half of it away? And why lie to me about it?'

He stood up. He towered over Billy like a monster in a horror film.

'Your mother and I have had about as much as we can put up with from you. Our family's never been in trouble before. We've never been liars. We've never had to be. Now we get you being brought home by the police, letters from the child welfare, people prying around to see we're looking after you properly. And now . . .'

His lips were wobbling. He looked away.

'I don't know what you're on about,' muttered Billy desperately.

'Don't you?' Dad's voice was much louder.

'There's no need to shout,' Billy said sulkily.

He really did shout now. 'Don't you tell me when there's any need for me to shout. I have to shout at you, you take no notice otherwise. You never listen.' He spat the last word out as if it was something nasty-tasting on the end of his tongue.

'You'll wake Mandy,' said Billy. 'And old Ma Wilson next door.' ('I heard your father giving you a talking-to, young man.' Cackle cackle. 'Better late than never, I always say.')

'Oh,' said Dad. 'So you're worried about Mandy and Mrs Wilson are you? That's wonderful, that is. What a considerate little . . .'

He was running out of steam. He hadn't shouted much, really, and he hadn't tried to hit him. Billy suddenly felt really scared.

'Come on, Billy, tell me. What's it all about?'

He talked quickly, like someone who thinks he's given you a fair chance to have your say and wants to stop wasting time. 'I'm going to count up to ten . . .'

Billy wondered if he could make it to the door before Dad caught him. If he got downstairs, got on his bike, got away, stayed out a couple of hours, Dad would cool down. It had happened before.

Dad must have seen him look in that direction. He stood up,

picked up the table and put it down again in front of the door. The glue nearly tipped over and he set it right. He had his back to Billy.

When he turned round he asked quietly, 'Have you been sniffing it?'

Billy nodded and waited to be bashed.

Nothing happened. Billy looked up. His dad was just standing there. His face had gone all funny and his arms hung by his side as if his muscles had collapsed.

His face was awful. It was like an old inner tube lying in a wrinkled heap on a garage floor.

Billy watched his dad grope his way on to the chair. He sat with its back between his legs, his head slumped on its top.

'Billy,' he said again, 'don't, *please*, ever do that again.'

He usually only said 'please' about things that didn't matter, or when Gran was around. But he didn't look as if this didn't matter. He'd be crying any minute.

'I don't see anything wrong with it,' said Billy.

'*You* don't see. No. You're too young.'

'It's just a laugh,' said Billy. 'Adults always want to stop kids enjoying themselves.'

Dad made a funny moaning noise and pushed his face into his knuckles. Billy could see the bald spot on the top of his head.

'Billy,' he said. The word came from behind his hands like a squeak from a door in another room. 'On Sunday night,' he went on, a bit more in his normal voice but still not quite right, 'I watched a programme on the telly. It was for teenagers, so, naturally' – this sarcastic bit sounded much more like the usual Dad – 'they showed it at eleven o'clock. Personally, I thought at the time that people your age shouldn't be allowed to see it anyway. Now I wish to God you had.'

He sat up and grabbed his hanky from his pocket and wiped his face. He missed a big damp patch on his right cheek.

'It was about teenagers who sniff glue, Billy. Ordinary, good-hearted boys, with decent parents. But they sniff glue.

37

One of them . . .' His voice wobbled and he stopped a minute. 'He might be you . . . This boy used to have a fishing rod, a rifle, a Walkman, a motor bike. All the things you want.

'He used to have them. Now he's sold them. To buy glue. He doesn't eat, he doesn't work. His house is a filthy mess, covered in streaks of glue he's spilt when he's . . . high on the stuff . . . He's a zombie, Billy, a complete and utter zombie. Is that what you want to be?'

'I wouldn't be as thick as that,' said Billy. It was typical. There was some stupid fool doing stupid things on the telly or in the newspapers and Dad thought you would be just the same.

'He can't help it, Billy. He doesn't know what he's doing.'

'Pull the other one,' said Billy. 'Course he knows what he's doing. He's doing it, isn't he?'

'He doesn't, Billy, he's drugged.'

Billy thought of not seeing Mandy when she'd come in. At least Dad didn't know about that.

'Anyway,' he said, 'I'm not gonna do it again. That's why I threw it away.'

'I pray God that's true, Billy.'

Billy sighed. His mum and dad didn't go to church or anything, but when they wanted to get at him they started talking about God.

'I'll tell you something else,' his dad added. 'If I get any hint you've done it again, the least little hint, then I'll be dropping you at school in the morning and your mother will fetch you home to lunch and collect you after school. You'll only go fishing when one of us can go with you. And you can forget that paper round. I mean it, Billy.'

'Mum won't want me home for lunch every day,' objected Billy. 'She goes to work, and bingo, and the shops . . .'

'She'll understand how important this is,' said his dad. 'It's a matter of life and death, Billy, life and death. I only hope I never have to tell her about this.'

He stood up, moved the table back to its place and swung the chair under it.

'You'd better get to bed now. Think about what I've said. If there's anything you want to talk to me about I hope you will. Choose a time when your mother isn't around. And keep quiet about it to Mandy as well. They've only just got over the last upset.'

Before he opened the door he looked back at Billy.

'One thing I want you to remember especially,' he said, all chokily: 'Whatever your mother and I do, however clumsy we are, we're doing it for your good.'

He went out.

Chapter Six

On Saturday morning it kept half-starting to rain, then stopping. There'd been wind and thunder in the night and now it was as if the weather had got the sulks after losing an argument.

Billy had to do his papers and then he was going fishing. At the shop there was a row on between Mr Thomas and a boy who'd delivered papers to three wrong houses on Friday.

The shop was in a little winding street just off the main bus route and lorries parked in it when they were delivering to the back doors of the big shops. Two were there when Billy came out and there was a queue stretching into the High Street, blocking two buses and some cars. Billy rode zig-zag through the lorries and cars, his bag full of papers swinging on one side, his fishing gear sticking out on the other. He nearly crashed into a man carrying a tray full of cream cakes into a posh café.

When he got to the tow-path and the last two houses on his round, the Colonel was snipping dead leaves out of his window boxes, and he had a tin of paint and a brush on the step. He must be going to paint his front door again. He was always doing something at the front of the house, and watching the boats and the people go past while he did it.

He stood to attention and saluted Billy, said, 'All present and correct, sir,' then took *The Times*. He looked at the front page, said 'Blasted Irish,' and put the paper on a stand thing just inside the door.

'Nasty night,' he said. 'Real snorter. Put my geraniums down for the count in the back there. Summer's over, I suppose.' The Colonel was still talking when Billy went next door and shoved *The Guardian* through the letter box. The door opened while he was doing it and the man who lived there came out, shouting over his shoulder. He crashed into Billy.

'I'll get the shop opened up. And you get a move on. Sorry, son, good morning, Colonel. Flowers surviving?' Without waiting for an answer he shouted through the door again. 'Marcia? Did you hear me?'

Billy heard something falling over in the house and a woman swearing. The Colonel was listening to what was going on just like Billy was. He winked at Billy, then shook his head and pretended to be shocked.

The window above the door slid up and the woman – Marcia, it must be – stuck her head out. When he saw her Billy wanted her to win the fight she was having.

'Would there be anything wrong,' she asked, and she sounded really fed up, 'in your being in the same room as me when we're talking?'

The Colonel was backing into his house, holding his finger up to his lips. Billy walked away along the tow-path. He heard the man say something and Marcia swearing again. Next thing the man passed him, going like the clappers, and turned up Water Lane. Billy decided he didn't like him.

Billy walked slowly along the tow-path pushing his bike. He heard Marcia swear again.

He repeated the name 'Marcia' to himself so that he'd remember it. Mum liked to listen to the gossip he brought home from his round. She told him off for being nosey, but she listened just the same.

Jake and Sharon were already fishing at the bottom of Water Lane. Sharon's rod was a kiddish thing that Billy wouldn't have been seen dead with, but he didn't mind showing her how to use it. She was waving it about now as if she was the music teacher at school trying to make them all sing louder.

Jake's wasn't very good, but at least it was a reasonable size. Mandy had said something once about Jake's rod being longer than Sharon's and Billy's being biggest of all and she'd wondered why the rest of them had laughed. She'd kept on at Sharon to explain, but she wouldn't while Billy and Jake were there. Billy had explained on the way home afterwards and she'd wrinkled her nose and said 'I think that's silly.' 'Why?' Billy asked. 'Because it's another word I can't say without you lot laughing. Like stick and prick and thing and . . . You just think you're big because you've got something I haven't.'

'Well I am.'

'Not.' And she'd punched him in the chest and jumped off and run beside him shouting, 'Billy's got a thing and he thinks he's big.'

She was at Brownies this morning.

When Jake and Sharon saw Billy they said 'Hi' but not much else, just looked at each other. When he asked them questions they would only say 'Yes' or 'No'. After a while Billy gave up. He didn't go away, but he moved a few feet along and left them to it. They seemed embarrassed about something.

Even when Billy caught a couple of bleak and they had a look before he threw them back, they didn't say much.

After a long time, the sun came out a bit and the water got a shine on it. A man with a stool and easel started to sketch the bridge. A sort of market was going on in a yard up some steps from the tow-path and there was a noise of people from there.

At half-past ten Sharon got a flask out of her bag. She always brought some coffee and enough plastic cups for all of them. She called Billy over, holding out a cup.

'Jake wants to say he's sorry,' she said, 'but he doesn't know how.'

'What for?' asked Billy.

'For what he said on Thursday.'

Billy shrugged. 'Doesn't matter,' he said. 'Forget it.' He grinned at Jake.

Jake still looked unhappy. The corner of his mouth kept moving as if there were words in there trying to get out.

'What's the matter with him?' Billy asked Sharon.

'He's sorry he called you a fool but he still hopes you'll stop mucking about with glue,' she said.

'Yeah,' said Jake.

42

Billy shrugged again and drank the coffee. 'Forget it,' he said again.

He knew that wasn't enough. They wanted a promise from him. 'I threw the can away,' he said.

Jake grinned for the first time since Billy had arrived. 'Great, man,' he said. 'That's great!' He punched Billy on the arm. Billy threw the empty cup to Sharon and chased him.

Jake ran to the circular seat around the tub with the tree in it and dodged backwards and forwards behind it. An old man asleep on the seat with his mouth open woke up and looked at them through his eyelashes. He moved his feet away from Billy's boots.

Jake shot away, nearly going over the edge into the river. He ran – and he could run very fast over a short distance – towards the bridge. Sharon laughed and shouted something as they passed her.

Jake disappeared up the steps to the road and Billy belted after him. Jake had stopped and flattened himself against the wall, and laughed like a drain when Billy fell over trying to stop and turn all in one.

They wrestled their way back to Sharon. She told them that while they'd been gone pike and tench and carp had been lining up to be caught but she'd had to send them away.

Chapter Seven

On Sunday Jake went to see his Aunty Josie. His mum and dad were at church. He waited for the bus outside the fried chicken place, leaning against a notice that said *Thank you for coming. Please put your litter in a bin.*

He went on the top deck of the bus, not because he smoked but because he liked to see where he was going. He sat right at the front, looking down on the cars and single-decker buses and the people hunched up against the wind.

The bus crawled through Thamesford even though it was Sunday and there wasn't much traffic. The Gas Board had dug up the roads, and all over the place there were ditches and piles of earth and broken concrete with warning signs sticking out of them. The yellow of the plastic pipes they were using to replace the old ones was the only colour anywhere.

He wondered how Josie would be.

Josie was his aunty, his mother's sister, but – and he had never told Billy or Sharon this – she was only nineteen. Jake was nearly as tall as she was, and when she made a joke of it and called him her boyfriend it didn't look totally stupid.

He hadn't told them she was a pop singer either. She wasn't famous, just a singer with a band that did gigs – that was what they called their jobs – in pubs and clubs round Wandsworth and Brixton and Lambeth. She said she didn't get much money, but she had enough to have a flat of her own in a house in Brixton and she used to have new clothes and records all the time.

It was a long way to Brixton from where Jake lived. He reckoned his mum and dad thought it wasn't far enough. Every time there was trouble in Brixton and pictures of blacks and police hitting each other on television, his parents got very upset and told him he was well out of it. And it was times like that they got on to him especially, about working hard at school and getting qualifications. 'You're lucky you live with us here,' they'd say. 'Down Brixton you're just one of thousands.'

When they talked like that, Jake always made jokes – not about Brixton, or being black, or getting a job, just jokes – and clowned around. They liked him to be happy. They thought that was the most important thing and it made them feel better. Anyway, whenever he was in any sort of trouble, a big toothy grin got him out of it, mostly.

It was only when Josie stopped living with their gran in Lambeth that Jake started visiting her. She asked him over to the flat one afternoon. He'd had a job getting his mum and dad to let him go. They thought Josie was wicked to leave Gran and that he was as bad as she was for wanting to accept her invitation. But they were afraid if they said 'No' he might disobey them and go anyway. Besides, no one else in the family ever went to see her, so they let him, and each time she invited him they asked him about what he'd seen when he got back. Later, after he'd gone to bed, he'd hear his mother on the phone to Gran, passing it all on.

He didn't tell them everything. He didn't lie, just answered the questions they asked him, without adding anything. 'What did you have for tea?' they'd start. 'Was there anybody else there?' 'Does she live by herself in the flat?' 'Does she ever send you away suddenly when the phone goes or somebody turns up?' He'd got very good at pretending not to see what was behind their questions. He didn't want to fight them about Josie but he didn't want to seem to be on their side against her.

Lately it had all got more difficult because she had changed. He'd noticed it first the same week as the two other worst things that had ever happened to him.

One was when Billy got caught by the police. Billy hadn't seemed to worry, but when Jake's mum and dad heard, they'd wanted Jake to stop seeing him. He'd talked them out of that by saying he'd be Billy's chaperone – a word he'd got out of a book they'd read at school – and that had made them laugh. But it had made Jake sick, just the same, the way Billy had shrugged it all off as if he'd done nothing wrong and the way adults carried on was nothing to do with him.

The second bad thing that week was when Sharon was helping him with some work on the bus after school. He'd asked her to explain some maths because he'd been mucking about in the class and now he had to understand it for homework. But, after she'd been talking a while, he'd started to watch a fight between two kids a couple of seats in front. She'd seen him not paying attention and said, 'Just turn that woolly head here will you?'

For a minute he'd hated her. Everyone on the bus must have heard and be laughing to themselves. Her saying that meant she thought he was thick and lazy, just like any other West Indian.

She'd realised straight away what she'd said, but neither of them had known how to get over it. He'd put his books in his bag and not done the work that night. The next day he got into trouble. He didn't look at her when it happened and he avoided talking to her for two days.

Then she'd turned up on the tow-path when she knew from Billy that he'd be there and talked to him non-stop until he couldn't sulk any longer. So it had been all right again. Except that now he wondered when something like that would happen again.

He'd been bothered about those two things when he went to see Josie that Sunday. He thought seeing her would cheer him up but he knew straight away when he got there that something was wrong. She was smoking, which she didn't usually do – she said it wrecked people's voices and lungs – and there was a bottle of gin open on the table.

In fact she was drunk and, when he asked her why, she just said – as if he must know what she was talking about – that glue was for kids. Gin was much better. He'd never realised that she'd been a sniffer. The gin seemed even worse. He'd never known anyone who got drunk. His mum and dad and gran didn't, because they were Pentecostalists. He'd always thought of alcohol as a kind of poison.

Listening to her had been strange and he hadn't liked it. It was as if she was really talking to herself and he just happened to be in the room.

One of the things he'd never told his parents was that, although Josie lived alone in the flat, she had a boyfriend called Emanuel, from the band, who was sometimes in bed with her when Jake arrived. He could see Josie wanted *him* to know about Emanuel but he couldn't decide whether he was supposed to tell his mum. So he didn't. He mentioned Emanuel sometimes but made him sound as if he wasn't important.

But now, Josie said, Emanuel had walked out on her. He'd told her that she was a Godless tramp and a whore and she'd destroy his soul if he had anything more to do with her. He was leaving the band to start another one. They would be travelling round singing religious songs as a backing group for a preacher – a righteous servant of God, Emanuel said. Emanuel could only pray that he would be forgiven the foul sins of the flesh he had committed with Josie and that she would be saved before she went to hell and got the punishment she deserved. And he'd let fly with a lot of stuff about fire and brimstone and burning lakes that Jake had heard at church sometimes.

While Josie was talking she got through two or three glasses of gin and she smoked one cigarette after another. When he left to go home he realised he stank of smoke. He'd tried to get rid of the smell by walking part of the way but it hadn't worked. He'd told his mother there'd been a lot of people smoking at Josie's place, making it sound as if Josie hadn't been. Then he realised his mum was more worried about him than about Josie, so he'd pretended to hide nicotine stains on his fingers from her and breathed into her face shouting, 'I stink of tobacco!' until she'd told him to stop being silly and sent him to bed.

Later, worse things had happened. Some of the cigarettes

Josie smoked didn't come out of a packet and smelt different from ordinary ones. And there were always pills round the flat. Some were in the sort of bottle with a label you got from a chemist, some weren't.

Talking to Josie got to be like working in a phone-in programme on the radio, listening to people's problems. Only, there was no doctor or studio expert to tell Josie what to do. Just Jake. She'd even talked about dying once. He hoped she wouldn't do that again.

The flat was near one of the roads that had been damaged in the riots in the summer. The people around knew Jake now and called out to him when they saw him. In a funny way he felt at home.

He went round the back of the house and up the steps to her entrance on the first floor. He knocked and went in and heard her calling, 'That you, Jake?'

'Yeah.'

When she came in she was wearing a tatty old dressing gown. She got thinner every week.

'Hi, Jake.'

'Hi.'

She didn't seem to be on a trip or anything. Just very tired. Her eyes looked red and her hand shook a bit but, compared to how she'd been, this was better.

She put one of his favourite records on the old record player she had now. He grinned. 'How's the band? Any gigs this week?'

She was standing by the window staring into the garden. It was windy out there.

'We did our last gig on Tuesday. The band's broken up. They're all starting with other groups.'

Jake didn't know what to say.

'Have you got another group?' he asked after a while, afraid of the answer.

'No. My singing's . . . gone off lately. No one wants me.'

She wasn't shouting or sounding sad or anything. Just

standing there, a small, thin shadow against the window and what was left of the light.

'I signed on at the Job Centre, Wednesday. Thought I might get something. Make a new start. But there's hundreds like me. Nobody needs them. I owe two weeks on the flat.'

'You could go and live with Gran.'

'No!' She shouted that, then dropped her voice again almost as if she hadn't noticed her own anger.

'That's what they want. Gran. Your mum and dad. The rest of them. Give up and go home. Admit I got it wrong. Say I'm sorry.'

She turned to him. 'Jake, you can't stay . . . Someone's coming. I only let you come because I wanted to say goodbye. You've been good to me.'

Jake had started to shiver. He'd thought she was all right, but this was worse than ever.

'Are you going away with him, this man?'

'Yes.'

'When are you coming back?'

'I don't know. You'll hear about it.'

She came over and pulled him to his feet. 'Off you go. There's a good boy. I've got to have a bath. Goodbye.'

And suddenly he was clattering down the steps and Josie was waving at him from the top with a really weird smile on her face.

He had to wait a long time for a bus and it was nearly an hour and a half before he got home. When he came in the door his mum was just putting the phone down. His dad was standing by her as if they'd both been talking to whoever it was. They were crying.

His mother rushed over to him and wrapped him in her arms with her head on his shoulder. Her tears ran down his neck. His father just stood there, looking as if he'd collapsed inside.

Chapter Eight

At the end of break on Tuesday morning Billy saw Sharon in the corridor.

'Where's Jake?' he asked her. 'I haven't seen him around.'

Sharon pulled him over to the wall. Someone whistled and she poked her tongue out at them.

'Haven't you heard?' she asked.

'No,' said Billy, uncomfortable because he was talking to her at school, in front of everybody. 'What?'

'He's been away because his aunty . . . died. On Sunday.'

'That's when he was going to see her,' said Billy.

'It was just after he left. He found out when he got home.'

Billy was puzzled. 'Why wasn't she in hospital then? You can't just die like that, with no one around.'

'She didn't just die,' Sharon said. 'She . . .' Sharon didn't seem to want to say what she was saying, '. . . cut her wrists. In the bath.'

'Did Jake see her do it?' asked Billy.

'I told you he found out when he got home, you thick,' said Sharon angrily. 'Anyway, don't you care? Jake's aunt's killed herself.'

He shrugged. 'I didn't know her. I can't help it. When's the funeral?'

'Thursday.'

'You going?'

'Yes. Mum's writing to the Head to get me time off.'

'Here he comes now,' said Billy. 'I'd better go.'

'We won't have any loitering,' said the high-pitched voice. 'You were due in your classes two minutes ago.'

Billy scarpered. There was no point getting into trouble when it wasn't your fault.

He didn't think very much during the rest of the day about

50

what Sharon had told him. He hoped Jake would be all right and would still be able to come fishing. He wondered how much mess Jake's aunt had made and who'd found her.

Last period they had Miss Richards. Billy had done his homework for once, but he'd got a lot of it wrong. The old bag didn't seem to have anything better to do than go on at him about how lazy he was.

'How do you expect to get on in life if your work's like this?' she shouted, waving his book. Everyone looked at him to see what he'd do. If teachers made him mad he answered back. The other kids liked to have a laugh without getting into trouble themselves.

He shrugged. He wanted to stay out of bother if he could. They might write home again.

'Answer me, Billy. I will not be ignored.'

'How can I ignore you when you're making all that noise?' he muttered. Someone laughed.

'I beg your pardon?'

She was coming down the row of desks towards him. Her glasses were nearly falling off the end of her nose and her voice had gone all deep because if she didn't make it do that when she shouted, it would go all squeaky instead.

'I said I'm not ignoring you.'

'Thank you very much. I suppose I should be thankful for that.'

He'd set her off now.

'Billy is not ignoring me. He's not doing his homework properly, he's not paying attention to my lessons, he's insolent and unpleasant, but he's not ignoring me. My life is worthwhile after all.'

She went back to the front of the room, then suddenly swung around and threw his book at him. It whooshed through the air, spinning like a Frisbee, hit him in the face and fell on to his desk.

'See me at the end of the lesson,' she said.

The rest of the period was very quiet. She only threw things when she was really angry. It didn't pay to upset her when she

51

was like that. The kids still talked about the time she'd slapped Jimmy Badger's face. Jimmy was very big, and a bully, a worse bully than Martin even, but she'd shut him up. No one ever dared to say anything about it to him.

Billy looked at the exercise he was supposed to be doing, but he couldn't see the point of all the effort. It was hard to get it right and it was hard to do it neat, and if you did it right and neat they 'encouraged' you by saying you should be able to do everything right and neat. That was stupid.

Miss Richards just sat at her table, staring at the back wall. She glared at anyone who breathed.

When the bell went, Billy waited for the others to go, then went up to the table. She looked at him and held out her hand for his book without saying anything. He had to find it and get it out of his bag, looking at her to see if he was doing the right thing. She looked at his homework again.

'I should keep you in,' she said, 'but I can't bear to sit here and look at my failure for another twenty minutes. Take this home and do it again. Bring it to me at the staff-room tomorrow morning.'

'I'm sorry, miss,' said Billy.

She sighed. 'Yes. Perhaps you are. But you'll be even sorrier in two or three years' time when you leave school with no qualifications and no one will give you a job.'

She shook her head as if a bird or something was sitting on it and she was trying to shake it off. 'It's not necessary, Billy. You don't have to be like this. You're not stupid.'

Billy shrugged. He knew she'd think he was being rude and taking no notice of her, but he didn't know what he was supposed to do to make things better. He couldn't be like Jake, just doing enough work to keep out of trouble, nor like Sharon, working all the time because she enjoyed it. There wasn't any way out. He wished Miss Richards would understand that.

'Go on,' she said, 'go home.'

He walked slowly to the door, but as soon as he was through it he ran as fast as he could to the bike sheds.

He was strapping his bag on the back of his bike when a shadow fell across it. He hadn't heard anyone behind him. There was only one person in the school who crept up on you like that.

Martin was not looking any friendlier than usual.

'I want my glue,' he said.

Billy had hoped that being suspended would make Martin give his can up as a bad job.

'Haven't got it,' he said.

'Sniffed it all?' Martin grinned nastily as if Billy wouldn't have done that because he didn't have the guts.

'No. Dad took it.'

Martin's eyes wobbled a bit in their sockets. 'Yeah?' he said.

'Took it last Thursday. He caught me with it. Well, he found out.'

'D'ya tell 'im where ya got it?'

'No.'

Martin relaxed a bit. 'No use to me if your dad's got it.'

'Well he has. I can't get it back.'

Martin took a step nearer to Billy. 'Then you'll have to buy me another one, won't you?'

'I'm not doing that,' said Billy. 'Why should I?'

'You'd better.'

'You gave it to me to get out of trouble. You know what the Head said he'd do to anyone he caught. You got off 'cos a me.'

'It was half-full.'

'Tough,' said Billy.

'You've sniffed it all, I bet. Silly Billy.'

'Haven't.' When Martin called him that he wanted Billy to lose his temper and hit him. Then he would smash Billy around and say it was Billy's own fault. So Billy ignored him and walked his bike towards the school gate. If he could get that far, the teachers in the staff-room would be able to see what was happening and he'd be able to get on and ride away from Martin.

Martin had him sussed out though, and moved faster to get in front. Billy thought he'd better risk being caught riding inside the school. He put his foot on the pedal, scooted a few quick steps and jumped on.

'Hey!' shouted Martin. Billy biked about twenty metres across the playground away from Martin, then started to circle towards the gate. Martin, who was slow-moving as well as big, lumbered to cut him off. When he could spare any breath he shouted threats at Billy.

Billy would have made it except that, just as he was passing the door that led from school to the bike sheds, it opened and Mr Scott came out. Billy nearly ran into him, and he jumped backwards, catching his heel on the low step in front of the door.

'Hey!' shouted Mr Scott.

Billy thought of just riding through the gate and scarpering. But he knew Mr Scott had seen who it was. Even if he hadn't, Martin would grass for sure. He slowed down in a big circle and jumped off in front of Mr Scott.

He stood holding his bike and staring at the ground while Mr Scott thought about what he was going to say.

Martin lumbered up, whooshing like a steam engine. 'I told him not to, sir,' he panted. 'I told him it was against the rules and he'd get into trouble, but he wouldn't believe me, sir.'

Mr Scott looked at Martin instead of Billy.

'Well,' he said. 'How very public-spirited of you. I must make sure that this unexpected act of good citizenship is suitably publicised.'

'Can I have a merit mark, sir?' Martin looked as if he really thought he might get one. Teachers who didn't know Martin always thought he was all right to start with.

Mr Scott knew Martin. 'No,' he said, 'you can't. The rest of the staff would never stop laughing at me. Now, Billy.'

Billy looked at the ground again. Mr Scott was wearing big yellow shoes that looked like Cornish pasties. There was a dirty mark near the toe of one of them, and a bit of yellow thread trailing over the edge on to the ground.

'You knew, because Martin here told you . . .' Martin did a great big grin. He thought he'd done something good and was

54

being praised for it. He was horrible. '. . . that it's against the rules to ride your bike in the school grounds.'

'I knew before he told me,' muttered Billy. He wasn't going to let Martin get away with that.

'I thought you might have.' Mr Scott's hand appeared under Billy's face, grabbed his chin and pulled it up. 'Look at me, Billy, when I'm talking to you. You knew you shouldn't do it. Why did you?'

If he got Martin into trouble, Martin would get a load of his mates and they'd do something to Billy when they caught him. But Billy didn't see why he should get into trouble to save Martin. Especially not now. He'd get hauled off to the Head. His name was on the list and anything he did wrong had to be reported to the Head straight away. His form teacher had told him. And the Head would say again that he was 'incorrigibly uncooperative' and he'd have to write to Billy's parents.

Anything would be better than that. He might be able to dodge Martin and his gang.

'Martin was mucking me about, sir. I was trying to get away from him.'

'Where are you going, Martin?' asked Mr Scott.

Martin was trying to slide through the door into the school. He came back.

'It's him broke the rules,' he said. 'I hain't done nothing wrong.'

'Humph,' said Mr Scott. 'And Brentford are top of the First Division.'

'No, they're not, sir,' said Martin. Then he realised.

Mr Scott looked at his watch. 'Six of one and half-a-dozen of the other,' he muttered. 'Listen, the pair of you. We're going to walk to the gate. Come on.'

They did that.

'Now. Billy. Get on your bike and get moving. Don't let me see you on it inside school again. Martin, you walk home, don't you?'

'Yes. Sir.'

'Good. Get walking. Off you go, Billy.'

'Thank you, sir,'

Billy biked home quickly. That was Martin out of the way until tomorrow.

Chapter Nine

But when he got home there was a note from his mum on the table. "Whoever gets in first please go and get some coffee. A big jar. Ta, Mum.' There was a five pound note there as well.

And when Billy got to the shops, who was hanging around there, looking ugly, but Martin. His dull, sluggy eyes lit up and he waddled over.

'How's me old mate Billy?' he shouted as Billy tried to sneak into the supermarket.

'Get off,' said Billy.

'I want my glue.' He said that quietly in case anybody heard. 'And I want it now. If I get it I might forget what you told Scott about me.'

'Get off,' said Billy. 'I'll call the police.'

'You do,' said Martin, 'and I'll nick something and say you was with me.'

'You'd be in trouble too.'

Martin grinned his evil grin. 'Makes no difference to me. *My* mum and dad don't care.' He kicked Billy's ankle, not very hard. 'Come on, what you come here to get?'

'Coffee,' muttered Billy.

'There it is. Over there. What you having, Snob's Blend or Roast Sawdust?'

Billy took the jar his mum wanted and paid at the check-out. Martin waited for him outside.

'Now,' he said. 'You've got some money, hain't that lucky? There's a shop you can buy my glue, right here.'

'I'm not going there,' said Billy. 'The man knows my dad. He'll tell.'

'Ngh.' Martin made a noise through his nose. What Billy said wasn't true, but Martin didn't know that.

'That's a pity,' said Martin. 'We'll have to go down Wool-worth's then, won't we?'

'I'm not going back in Woolworth's with you,' said Billy quickly. 'They'd send for the cops soon as they saw us.'

'Well, you're just going to have to go in here then.' Martin sounded wild. When he got like that he'd clout you one that'd smash your face up like hamburger meat. Billy had seen him do it. And he wouldn't care that people were around to see. He didn't know what he was doing when he got wild, everybody said so.

Martin was crowding him, driving him towards the shop door.

'I'll look after your bike,' he said. 'Get in there and get the glue.'

'What you want it so badly for?' Billy was trying to hold him off. The shops would shut soon.

'What ya think? Makes me feel good, that's why.'

He was snarling a lot. Maybe if this went on long enough someone would interfere.

There was a sudden sharp pain in Billy's ankle. Martin had kicked him again, much harder.

'It's dangerous,' Billy said desperately. 'A boy killed his gran when he'd been sniffing. It was in the paper.'

'Me gran's dead already. Old bag probably deserved it anyway.'

Billy was keeping an eye on Martin's feet now and he managed to dodge the next kick.

'Hurry up,' Martin went on. 'It's nearly closing time.' He waited until a gang of schoolgirls had giggled past and three old ladies had wondered whether they had time to visit the library before a bus came. Then he stuck his piggy eyes up close to Billy and said, 'You just get me my glue an' you can get off home to drink your coffee. An' I'll go down the cemetery an' watch dead people dancing on the graves and flowers growing out of the headstones.'

'It didn't do that to me,' said Billy. 'I didn't see anything.' Not even Mandy standing in the doorway, he thought.

'Yah!' sneered Martin. 'You're a bottler. Always were. Little creep. Think you're tough, but you're not. You're as wet and weak as the tea-bags they use in the staff-room. Now *get in there.*'

Billy gave up. He'd have no ankles left at this rate. And Martin would be along with his mates tomorrow. He shoved his bike into Martin's hands and walked into the shop. He reckoned Martin wanted the glue more than he'd want to nick the bike.

There was a rack of red tins by the counter. *Confidence: the glue that stays stuck.* And you stay stuck on, thought Billy.

He picked up a can and put it on the counter with some money.

'What are you wanting this for, sonny-boy?'

Billy looked up. The Pakistani owner of the shop was smiling down at him. He was holding the can in both hands as if it was a cup that would break if it was dropped.

'Me dad's putting some tiles down in the kitchen,' gabbled Billy. He hadn't thought of saying that until he was asked.

The Pakistani didn't move, apart from making his eyes go narrow.

'I am thinking,' he said, 'that there are many foolish boys who are playing silly tricks because they have been sniffing this substance.'

'Don't know what you're talking about,' said Billy. 'Me dad just asked me to get it 'cause he's putting some tiles down in the kitchen. On the floor,' he added.

'I am not thinking he would be putting them down on the ceiling,' said the shopkeeper. 'Your father gave you this money to pay for the glue?'

'Yeah,' said Billy. He looked out through the window to see if Martin was still there with the bike.

'Are you afraid of something?' asked the shopkeeper.

'Nah,' said Billy. 'Me mate's out there looking after me bike.'

The shopkeeper's eyes followed Billy's. Martin seemed to be trying to keep out of sight.

'Your mate,' said the shopkeeper. 'I know this boy. He is not someone I would be wanting to be my mate. He is a nasty boy.'

'He's all right,' said Billy.

'I am sorry to say that you are wrong there,' said the shopkeeper. 'There are many businessmen in this parade who have caught him stealing from their shops. I am glad, to speak for myself, that he is looking after your bike outside and not coming in.'

'Can I have the glue, please?' said Billy. 'Me dad's in the middle of the job and me mum wants to cook the tea.'

'He would have been wiser to wait until cooking was finished for the night.' said the shopkeeper.

'I'll tell him,' said Billy.

Very slowly, looking at Billy all the time as if he was trying to hypnotise him, the shopkeeper rang up the price on his cash register and gave him his change. He put the can into a white plastic bag with *Do It Yourself and Be Proud* printed on the side. It was the name of the shop.

Billy went to the door, waving the bag in his hand. 'Here you are . . .' he said. The words went dry in his mouth. His dad was there, talking to Martin. He had Mum's note in his hand. He must have come to get the coffee.

'Billy.' His dad looked at him. 'Martin tells me he's looking after your bike for you while you're in there. What are you buying? I see you've got the coffee already.' The supermarket bag was in Billy's other hand.

Billy couldn't think what to say. Whatever he came out with, his dad wouldn't believe it when he found the glue.

He heard the Pakistani shopkeeper's voice behind him.

'Are you this boy's father?'

'Yes,' said Billy's dad.

'And are you in a hurry to finish putting tiles down on your kitchen floor, may I ask?'

Billy's dad gaped. Martin had leaned the bike against the shop window and was sneaking away.

60

'I think, Sir, and I am most sorry to say it, that your son is a most accomplished liar. He has been telling me . . .'

Billy dropped the glue and the coffee on the ground. 'Martin made me get it,' he shouted. 'I don't want it. It's nothing to do with me.'

He side-stepped around his dad, grabbed his bike, pushed it to the road, jumped on and rode off at high speed.

Chapter Ten

When it got dark, Billy went home. He knew if he was out after that his dad might ring the police.

He put his bike in the shed and walked up the path to the back door. His mum had heard him coming and was waiting in the kitchen. She grabbed him and hugged him a bit.

Then she said, 'Your father's not angry, Billy. He understands.'

Billy looked at her. He had to pull himself away. He put his bag down and leaned against the back of the kitchen door.

'I wasn't buying it for myself,' he said.

'We know. Your father talked to the shopkeeper . . .'

Billy wondered what the shopkeeper had said. He looked at the kitchen floor. It could do with smartening up.

'I'm sorry if you were worried,' he said. 'I just hung about in the park.' That wasn't quite true. He'd stayed on his bike almost the whole time, keeping an eye open for Martin. It had been quite cold, because he didn't have a coat or anything and, what with biking all the time, he was terrifically hungry now. He hoped Mum had kept something for him. He looked at the oven. It was on.

She followed his eyes. 'You go in and sit down and tell your dad where you've been,' she said. 'I've got something nice for you here, if it hasn't spoiled.'

He went through. Mandy was watching the telly with the sound turned down so you could hardly hear it. She looked up at him and waved. He grinned at her. Dad was still at the table, reading the paper.

'Hallo, Billy,' he said. 'Glad you made it.'

'Hallo,' said Billy, cautiously. You couldn't always tell from what he said how he was going to be. And Mum didn't always get him right either.

'Where've you been?'

'In the park.' Billy got himself a knife and fork and sat down opposite him.

'You must be cold. And hungry.'

'Yeah.'

'Say "Yes," please, Billy.'

'Yes.'

Dad put the paper down. 'That boy Martin . . . Was it him gave you the glue last week?'

'Yeah. Yes.'

Billy's mum came in with a plate. She was holding it with oven gloves. 'Careful,' she said, 'it's hot.'

The plate had faggots and Smash and carrots on it. They were a bit dry and brown at the edges but they looked good just the same. She put the plate in front of him, kissed his hair and went back to the kitchen. Then she stuck her head through the door again. 'Cuppa tea, Dad?'

'Yes, please. We could all do with one, I think,' said Dad. He went on, quietly, to Billy, 'He was after you to get it back, I suppose.'

'Yes.'

'You could have sent him to me.' He didn't really sound as if he believed that.

'He wouldn't've come. He'd just belt me until I got it for him.'

'Um.' He thought for a bit while he watched Billy laying into the faggots. 'Well, I'm not going to give it to you to take back to him at school.'

Billy was glad about that. If he took the can to school he was sure to get caught somehow. Martin might even make sure he did. But he wished Martin had it back so that he'd leave Billy alone.

'Do you know where he lives?'

'Somewhere near the station.'

'Um. Perhaps I could get the address from the school. I think I should give the glue to his father.' Then he looked quickly at Mandy to see if she was listening.

63

'His dad's gone off. And his mum's hardly ever there.'

'Um.'

Billy pushed his plate away just as Mum came in with the tea. Dad said, 'Tell you what.' He got a handful of change from his pocket and counted some out. 'I reckon there's about that much worth left in the tin.' He thought a bit then added twenty more pence to the pile. 'He might say there was more there than I think there was. If he bothers you, give him that. If he doesn't, I'll want it back in a few days. Tell him, if he wants the stuff and not the money he'll have to come and see me.'

Billy took the money. It might work. At least Dad was trusting him for once.

'Incidentally, Billy . . .' Dad was talking again. 'I had to tell your mother what's been causing all this bother.'

'Yes,' said Billy, looking at his mum.

She said 'We'll forget all about it, shall we, Billy?' and smiled brightly. 'You won't do it again, will you?'

'No,' said Billy.

'There's my good boy.'

Chapter Eleven

Sharon went with her mother to Josie's funeral at the Pentecostal Church. It was crowded, mainly with West Indians. Some of the choir had got time off work to come and they were ready in their blue robes. Sharon's mother said that folk were making a special effort, not so much because of Josie but because Jake's mum and dad and gran were such respectable and well-liked people. If it hadn't been for one of their friends being led of the Lord to go round and try to talk Josie back on to the straight and narrow, she might still be lying there.

Just before eleven o'clock the organ started to play sweet, creepy music. Sharon shivered. Four men in suits, with black ties, came through the door at the back of the church, carrying the coffin. Everyone went quiet and stood up. The men walked down the aisle, balancing the coffin on their shoulders, followed by Jake's mum and dad, and his gran, who was leaning on Jake's arm. (His mum had told Sharon's the night before that they weren't sure he'd be there, he was so upset.) His face was all funny, as if he'd stuck a bit of cardboard in his mouth to keep it in shape. He didn't look at anybody.

Sharon looked at the coffin. It was tiny. She'd never seen one before and she couldn't imagine anyone shut, nailed down, inside it. She started to work out how long it actually was, it was so much smaller than she expected. Then she wondered if that was rather an awful thing to be doing. She was glad it wasn't anyone she knew.

She looked across at Jake as everyone sat down. He had pulled out his handkerchief and put his face in it and his mother was saying something to him. After a while he sat up and stared straight ahead. Sharon thought he might be trying not to see the little box that held his aunty.

In the meantime, the minister had come on to the platform.

He was a big man who normally smiled a lot. He put his Bible and hymn book down on the reading desk in the middle of the front of the platform and looked slowly round at everybody.

'Brothers and sisters,' he said. 'It is human to be sad when someone we know and love is taken away from us. God, in his mercy and wisdom, has given us each other so that we may be comforted when the time of sorrow is upon us. We have come here today to enfold in our arms of love these our grieving friends. God is good, brothers and sisters. He will not leave us to suffer alone.'

Sharon thought of what Jake had told her, when they went round to his place on Tuesday, about how Josie had been just before she killed herself, and she wondered. Of course, Josie had *wanted* to be alone. No one had forced her to be.

Everyone was looking up a hymn in the book.

Amazing grace! How sweet the sound
That saved a wretch like me!
I once was lost . . .

Sharon couldn't sing because her throat had gone all swollen when she saw Jake with his handkerchief. The rest of them after a shaky start, were singing as if, by singing loudly, they could bring Josie back again.

Chapter Twelve

On Thursday evening at about eight o'clock Marcia slung her skates around her neck and set off for the ice rink. She had on her black track-suit trousers and, instead of the top, a quilted jacket with some extra pockets not provided by the makers.

When she and Brian started their night-time business, the ice rink had been their first outlet. In those days, Marcia had taken risks, choosing people she thought were possible customers and buttonholing them – in the changing rooms, in the café and the bar, on the ice, in the gallery seats as they watched. Even, once, in the queue for tickets at the entrance.

Now, after two years, she wondered how she had failed to be caught. Beginner's luck, Brian had said it was. He'd told her to be more careful, to take it slowly and easily. They were trying to establish a business, not to live on the razor's edge. As far as he was concerned they were in it for the money. He didn't even smoke much.

She realised that to get her kicks that way was to put others at risk besides herself. She changed her method, and turned up at the rink only once every two or three weeks.

She walked along the unlit part of the tow-path towards the rink. Brian had urged her many times to use the safely lighted streets. 'What if some maniac assaults you along there?'

'He'll get one in the eyes from my skate blades and one in the crotch from my knee.'

'I'm not worried about you,' he said bluntly. 'I know you can defend yourself. But what if your jacket gets torn while you're doing it?'

There was a short queue at the ticket window. An elderly man with a pointed beard paying for a party of six small boys. A party of six teenagers, none of whom she knew. Some of them might be possibilities. Two young couples, together.

She occasionally supplied one of the men and when he saw her he made a gesture with his head and hands which meant 'See you inside.' There was nobody much behind her. A priest with some kids who must be from his youth club, and two fair-haired children with their parents.

In the changing rooms she made her first sale. A young actress who sometimes appeared in television commercials asked her for a light for an ordinary cigarette and while they were fiddling with that they exchanged two small plastic bags and money.

When she put her skates on, she remembered her father taking her skating when she was a little girl, buying her first skates for her one Christmas. She didn't see him often now. He was very old-fashioned.

Chapter Thirteen

When Mandy's dad asked her and Billy, while they were having tea, if they'd like to go to the ice rink, they could hardly say 'Yes, please,' for a minute, they were so surprised. When they did get over the shock and started shouting and knocking the table, Mum told them to calm down or they'd stay at home, but Mandy could see both Mum and Dad were pleased, especially by the way Billy's face lit up.

In the car, Mandy and Billy bounced around so much on the back seat that Dad nearly got angry. He said they'd cause an accident.

While they were waiting in the queue for tickets, Billy pulled Mandy's anorak and nodded at a lady who was in the queue in front of them. 'Remember I said I saw someone having a row last Saturday when I delivered their paper? That's her.'

'Has she recognised you?' Mandy asked him. The lady was just standing there looking around at everyone without nodding or smiling.

'Nah,' said Billy. 'They never do.'

Billy looked at the lady a lot. Mandy began to think he might fancy her. Billy never had anything to do with girls apart from Mandy and Sharon, and with Sharon it was only because she liked fishing and she was a friend of Jake's.

Poor Jake. It was his aunty's funeral today.

'She's called Marcia,' said Billy, still looking at the lady. He said it as if there was something special about the name. Mandy laughed at the poshness that had got into his voice.

'*Mah*ciah. My deah *Mahh*ciah,' she said.

'Shut up,' muttered Billy. 'She'll hear you.'

When Marcia got her ticket and went into the ladies' changing room, Billy seemed to forget her and think about skating again. He showed Dad where there was a sign pointing to 'Skate Hire' and told Mandy where to look to see into the rink.

They got their tickets and skates and Mum helped Mandy put hers on. Mum wasn't skating, although they tried to make her. She'd just sit and watch them bruising their situpons, she said.

When Mandy got to the rink she saw Billy already flat on his back on the ice. Dad said he'd rushed on as if it was an ordinary playground. He wouldn't do that again. He went to Billy and picked him up by his hands, then walked backwards with Billy holding his hands and trying to make his skates slide smoothly. Dad looked as if he really knew what he was doing.

'Has Dad been here before?' Mandy asked her mum.

Mum gave her a funny smile. 'We used to come here a lot.' Then, as if she was giving away a big secret: 'Actually, I met your father here.'

'Why did you stop coming?'

'We had Billy, then you. There wasn't time, or . . . Anyway we want you and Billy to enjoy yourselves.'

'Can I start now?' asked Mandy.

She hadn't any idea what to do. If Billy had fallen over she was sure she would. But most people seemed to manage. They found it so easy they looked as if they were standing still most of the time.

'I'll hold you,' said Mum. 'No, better, I'll walk along here behind the barrier and you can grab the barrier or me if you want to. Try to move smoothly.'

Mandy stepped on to the ice and fell over straight away. The third time she looked up at Mum's upside-down laughing face she wanted to cry, but she knew if she did that Mum would say 'There, there,' and pat her as if she was a kid. She pulled herself up and stood with her back to the barrier watching the other people whizzing past.

A voice over the loudspeakers asked them to go off the ice. Mum said there was going to be an exhibition. Mandy and Billy watched until they got bored, then Billy turned his back on the rink. Mandy noticed he was staring at something. It was Marcia, talking to a man. She gave him something.

'Mahciah, Mahhciah,' said Mandy softly, but Billy took no notice. He was watching and thinking.

After a while there was another announcement and everyone went back on the ice.

When Dad came across and said it was time to go, Mandy and Billy wanted to stay, but when they were promised they could come again they shut up. Dad took them to have a coffee in the café before they went home.

While they were drinking it, Billy dropped something and scrambled under the table to find it. Mandy got down to help him, but he wasn't really looking for anything at all. He was spying on another table in the next row. Mandy saw some hands and something small and shiny being passed between them, she couldn't see what. Billy made a sign that she was to keep quiet.

She sat on her chair again and looked at the other table. There was only one person there now, a man, just finishing his coffee. The other person who'd been there was walking towards the door. Black trousers. A quilted jacket. Marcia.

Mandy wondered if Billy was getting a crush on her. She'd tease him about it when they got home. Better, when they were out fishing. He'd hate it if Sharon and Jake knew.

Chapter Fourteen

I'm not interested,' said Marcia.

Brian, who was driving, looked angry. They were on their way to the party after she'd finished at the rink. Brian was telling her about John's latest idea for expanding the business. It was to start importing heroin.

'Hash is one thing,' she said. 'Heroin is another. People can die from it – quite quickly. And horribly. You remember last year when that Irish girl from the rink went on to it. Half the other customers wanted out. They were scared. Rightly.'

'You can't win them all,' said Brian. 'We're in business. Car salesmen don't feel guilty about road deaths. Brewers don't cry themselves to sleep because of alcoholics. They pretend they do, but they've been told to by their public relations people. And what about the cancer manufacturers? We've all got something to sell and we sell it. How people use it is their own affair.'

'We're not in this just for the money.'

'I am. And so is John. He wants to make a lot of money in a short time, then live well. So do I.'

'You used to talk differently. What was it? "I believe in free use of the resources of the earth. The law is a conspiracy to deny people legitimate pleasure. Everyone has an equal right to be zonked out."'

'That's right.'

'But if we are only after money, you know what we have to do. Go for the kids. Start them on grass. Then pills. And so on. Give them what will kill them when we've had all the money they've got or can steal. Work towards a country full of hopheads mugging and murdering so that they can stay stoned.'

'You're exaggerating. Drug addiction comes in people, not

in syringes. But, in any case, we haven't much choice. John says we must go with him or be squeezed out. We're amateurs, he says. Especially you. "The beautiful secret agent", is what he calls you, "operating under the noses of the police. The elegant young woman of the world who knows her way round the dens of vice. The middle class tripper in the underworld. The friendly neighbourhood grocer".'

Marcia didn't reply. What Brian was saying meant that something she had always seen as a possibility might happen a lot sooner than she'd expected. She would have to ditch him before he ditched her.

When they arrived, the party was in full swing.

PART TWO

Chapter Fifteen

At about the same time, at a jetty on the west coast of Scotland, Brian's friend Hugh and their local man, old Mac, were hurrying to get Hugh's van loaded. It was so quiet there, ten miles from the nearest town, that every footstep on the gravel between jetty and road sounded as if it must be heard for hundreds of yards.

They spoke only in whispers, Mac heaving the cardboard cartons up from the rowing boat and Hugh stacking them neatly in the van. He took note – because, of course, he had to know – that they were marked *Powdered Potato: one hundred packets*. Once, when some illiterate fool had been allowed to do the job, it had been *Mushrom Soop*.

The last carton in, he dropped a jacket and holdall casually on top and shut the doors. He handed over a fat envelope, and within seconds Mac was invisibly rowing back to the off-shore island where he lived alone, keeping an eye on a few cattle for some mainland farmer. It would be a month before he again took the motor boat out into deep water to meet another freighter and relieve it of part of its cargo. Meanwhile, during the day, he'd mind beasts only a little hairier and less talkative than himself, and smoke his foul old pipe and drink horribly strong tea at night.

Hugh grinned to himself in the darkness, got into the van and drove off.

He travelled south at an easy seventy miles per hour, stopping at about two-thirty for a pie at an all-night café. He used a different café every trip; he didn't want to be recognised as a regular.

When he came off the M1 in North London there was hardly any traffic. He drove round the North Circular Road, leaving it eventually about half a mile from the derelict church which was a television repairman's workshop, and their warehouse on the side.

It was then that things started to fall apart.

Two blocks from the church Hugh noticed a flickering light behind the houses and heard sirens. At an intersection ahead of him he saw a fire engine and a police car cross his path in quick succession.

He slowed down, then pulled in before he reached the corner to think through the situation. Really there was nothing to stop him driving to the church and unloading. The police would be busy with the fire, road accident or whatever and wouldn't have time to spare to ask him what he was doing at this time of night or inspect the contents of the van.

But it would be silly to take risks.

But, again, there was nowhere else he could dump the stuff. There was no way he was going to leave it in his van.

He found he was panicking a bit. In the eighteen months they'd been operating they'd never had a whisper of trouble and he'd got used to the idea that it would always be easy.

He drove at normal speed to the street where the church was and turned into it. A policeman stepped into the road in front of him and held up a white-gloved hand. Hugh put his head out.

'I'm sorry, sir. This road's closed.'

'Oh,' said Hugh. 'I've just realised I'm in the wrong street anyway. I want . . .' and he named one he knew was several blocks away.

'In that case, sir, your best plan is to turn here, go left at the end . . .'

Hugh listened to what he already knew and tried to see what was going on further up the road. There were more policemen, quite a few more. They seemed to be knocking at all the houses in the street. Lights were going on and people were coming to doors.

Two fire engines were just visible, but smoke was billowing

thickly across the road. Whatever it was burning was well away. He hoped it wasn't the church.

The copper finished talking and Hugh thanked him. He moved the gear lever into reverse and asked casually, 'What's going on?'

'Fire in a store shed up here, sir. Next to the church, and we've been informed that there may be explosive and inflammable chemicals in the shed. We're evacuating houses to be on the safe side. The church roof is smouldering a bit already. So, if you don't mind, sir . . .?'

Hugh took the hint. 'Of course, officer, thank you.'

This was trouble. If there was any of the stuff left in the church, it might be found as a result of this. In any case he couldn't unload the van. If the church caught fire with stuff inside it . . .

He drove for ten minutes, putting as much distance as he could between himself and the fire. Then he found a phone box and dialled Brian's number. It was not up to Hugh to sort this out by himself, whatever Brian might say.

Chapter Sixteen

On Saturday morning Billy had an early breakfast. He gave Mandy a double as far as the bridge, then they walked to the paper shop. He was letting her go on the paper round with him to push the papers through the doors. She wanted to do a paper round herself, but Mum always said no, she was too young, the law wouldn't let her at her age. Anyway, you never knew who would be around at that time in the morning and it wasn't safe. Mandy wanted to know why and Mum said she was too young to understand. Mandy asked Billy what she meant one day when Sharon and Jake were there and between them they told her about flashers and rapists and perverts. Mandy thought people like that must be silly.

It took longer than usual to do the round because Mandy folded the papers very carefully and pushed them right through the letter boxes, even though it wasn't raining. She'd heard Dad giving Billy lectures on how to deliver papers when their boy hadn't pushed theirs through properly on a wet day and part of the paper was all soggy and you couldn't read it because it was just a grey mess. She'd look at each paper, too, before she folded it, even read some of it if Billy let her.

But they got to the tow-path while it was still quite early. The Colonel was just going out for his walk and when he saw Mandy helping he made a joke about Women's Lib and told Billy to watch it or she'd take over. 'The ladies run the world these days,' he said. 'Look at the Prime Minister. Frightens me to death,' he said.

Billy just grinned, the way he always did when the Colonel or anyone made jokes, but Mandy said, 'And there's the Queen as well.'

'Shut up Mandy,' said Billy.

The curtains were still drawn in Brian and Marcia's house. Mandy pushed the paper through.

The Colonel waited to walk along the tow-path with them. 'No sign of life in there,' he said. 'Exhausted after being up so early yesterday, I shouldn't wonder.'

He told them he'd seen Brian and Marcia up and about before breakfast yesterday, unloading a van at the warehouse in Water Lane. They'd seemed to be in a great hurry, he said.

'Is that *Mahcia* you're talking about?' Mandy asked. Billy wanted her to shut up because he didn't want her telling the Colonel what she thought about him and Marcia. It wasn't true, anyway. But when the Colonel said, 'Bit of all right, our Marcia,' and laughed in that funny way that was like a snort, Mandy just looked at Billy and didn't say anything.

By the slipway at the bottom of Water Lane Billy chained his bike to the railings and set up his fishing gear. The Colonel watched for a while before wandering off. Mandy went with him a little way.

Billy threw out some groundbait and made his first cast. Someone who'd hired a boat from the jetty on the other side of the bridge rowed downstream through one arch of the bridge and tried to turn and go back through the other. They didn't have much clue what they were doing. Billy laughed when the current made them miss the gap and run into one of the pillars of the bridge.

Mandy came back and crouched beside him.

'Caught anything?' she asked.

'Course I have,' said Billy. 'Didn't you see? Seals, porpoises, sharks, whales, the lot. An' a couple of bleak. Threw them all back.'

'Silly,' said Mandy. 'I just wanted to know.'

Girls were like that. Most of them. Mandy had been where she could see him the whole time since they got there. If he'd caught anything, he'd have had to strike, and play it, and get it on to the bank with the landing net, and weigh it on his scales when he'd got it off the hook, and throw it back, and write the date, time and weight in a little notebook he kept. She would

81

have seen all that happening for sure and come rushing back all excited and shouting to get in the way. None of that had happened, but she asked her feeble question just the same.

'All I've caught this morning is an underweight sister,' said Billy. 'An' if she wriggles and jumps about too much, I'll chuck her back in the water where she belongs.'

She screwed up her face the way she did when she was going to ask Dad what a budget was or why factory workers were on strike or being sacked.

'What was Marcia doing at the ice rink on Tuesday?'

'Dunno,' said Billy, but he felt himself blushing. He could never lie properly. It always got him into trouble. 'Shut up all these questions or I'll make you go to the bridge and back.'

'That's not fair. I'm not stopping you fishing.'

'Can't concentrate with you jabbering.'

Mandy stuck her tongue out at him. He reeled in his line, looked at the bait and cast again.

'What was she doing under the table?' asked Mandy after keeping quiet for a couple of minutes. 'She was giving somebody something, wasn't she?'

'Might've been.'

'What?'

Billy shrugged.

Mandy screwed up her face in a different way, as if she was going to cry. 'Why won't you tell me?' she asked. 'You saw her. You were trying to see what she was doing, you followed her around all night.

'You fancy her,' she shouted suddenly. 'That's why you won't say. *Mah*cia!'

Billy swung round at her. That made him pull his rod suddenly, which gave him the excuse he needed. 'Look,' he shouted, 'you're disturbing me! Walk to the bridge and back.'

'Only because you wouldn't tell me.'

She walked away from him, turning her head sometimes, sticking her lips out at him. He pretended not to see her.

He felt all hot. He didn't bother much about girls. He talked about them at school of course. He looked at dirty magazines under the desk. He clenched his fist and banged his elbow and pumped his arm up and down, the same as the rest did. He dreamed about them sometimes. But he didn't hang around them in the playground and never thought about them unless they acted stupid in class.

But Marcia made him feel funny, just seeing her. She made him think of films when there was kissing and sex. He didn't want her to notice him looking at her – that idea scared him – but he wanted to look. At the ice rink he had worked out all sorts of reasons for skating to the places where she was.

Following her around he'd seen her passing things to people. Little bags. Once, under the table, when Mandy had seen. Once, in the middle of the ice, when she'd been standing talking very close to another lady. She'd seemed to have her hand in the other lady's pocket.

Billy had heard about stuff being passed around at rinks and discos and parties. Somehow the thought that Marcia might be doing that had made him feel very sad, like if he'd heard Mandy using really awful swear-words or Dad had hit Mum. Now he thought about it again he felt as if he might spew.

He managed to swallow the lump in his throat and hold down the swelling feeling in the top of his chest. When Mandy came back he was sitting there just fishing as if everything was all right.

'Here's Sharon and Jake,' Mandy said.

Chapter Seventeen

Billy didn't know what to say to Jake. He hadn't seen him since his aunty had committed suicide. Sharon had told him about the funeral but she'd just said that Jake and all his family were very upset and that she hadn't talked to him.

He looked all right now. They all said 'Hi' and Jake and Sharon got their tackle set up and made their first casts. While that was happening they were just talking about the weather and the water and if there would be any fish around.

Then Mandy started telling Sharon about something that had happened in school the day before. The teacher had said something to her and without thinking she'd said 'Yes, Mum,' back. Other people had laughed and she'd been embarrassed. 'I felt like killing myself,' she said.

Everyone went quiet. Sharon nearly said something, but didn't. Mandy blushed and bit her lip. All of them looked at Jake, then thought they shouldn't and looked away again. There were tears in Mandy's eyes, Billy could see, but she was forcing herself not to cry.

Jake went on fishing as if he hadn't heard. Billy looked at Sharon and they both looked at Mandy. Then they fiddled with bits of tackle, reeled in and cast again. Mandy couldn't do that, so she just sat staring across the river, with her lip going white around where she was biting it.

'You're all right,' said Jake. 'You can make mistakes and it doesn't matter, because people like you.'

'I didn't mean it, Jake, honest,' said Mandy, all in a rush. Then a couple of tears that had been sticking in the corners of her eyes loosened and rolled down her face. She rubbed them away.

'Your mum and dad and gran cared about Josie, Jake,' said Sharon.

'I didn't say they didn't,' said Jake. 'But Josie hated them.'

They were quiet again. Billy noticed that both Sharon and Jake had stopped talking about his 'aunty'. He'd found out himself from a newspaper that Josie had been a pop singer and was only nineteen. Now, of course, he wanted to know more about her, but he couldn't very well ask. He thought Marcia was older than that, about twenty-four, he reckoned.

'It's stupid,' said Jake. 'Josie just wanted to live her own life. And it was all right until . . . a while ago. But Gran just thought she wanted to get away from her to have men in and get drunk all the time. They never believed anything she said unless it was about having her own way. They think what happened was what had to happen if she left home. They're all sad about it, sure, but you can see them thinking they were right and she was wrong.'

'Was she on drugs before she moved?' Sharon asked.

'No.' Jake said that, then he seemed to think about it. 'Well . . .' He jiggled his line a bit but didn't reel it in. 'She started on drugs – real drugs, not glue and booze and fags – a few months ago . . . Well, it was a few months ago I found out about it. It's awful finding out something like that about someone you like.'

Billy saw the white streak of glue across the brown leather of his boot. He would have that as long as he had the boots, maybe.

'After that she didn't bother to hide it any more. She smoked stuff and she had pills and syringes in the flat. That was when she started to sell her records and things.'

'To buy more drugs,' said Mandy.

'Yeah,' said Jake.

Billy wished Mandy hadn't said that. You could tell without her asking. Kiddish.

'Poor Josie,' said Sharon.

Jake reeled in his line. 'Yeah,' he said. 'But she's out of it now, isn't she? She's left the mess behind her for other people to clear up.'

The rest of them stared at him in surprise.

He looked at Billy. 'Don't you get started on the stuff,' he said. He sounded as if he would hit Billy any minute. 'If you do, and you end up like her, I'll, I'll, I'll kill you.'

Billy laughed. He didn't mean to, he didn't *want* to, but he couldn't help it. 'Be a bit late, wouldn't it?' he said.

'It's not a joke,' said Jake.

'No, it isn't,' said Mandy. 'You leave it alone. And stay away from Marcia.'

Suddenly they were all shouting at each other. Billy was telling Mandy to shut up. Jake was shouting at Billy about what he'd do to him if he became a junkie. And Sharon was trying to calm them all down.

Some adults went past in a group and stared at them. That made them shut up because they didn't want other people to hear what they were saying.

'Just listen to those kids,' said one of the adults. 'Not a care in the world!'

A while after that Jake had a bite and they all got excited. Too excited, because he lost it. Then Sharon's line tightened as well, but that got away too.

Then Mandy got bored and started teasing Billy because he'd had no bites. She said the others were teaching him how to fish. He told her she was a silly kiddish girl and she ought to shut up.

Making sure she was well out of reach, Mandy asked him, 'Is Marcia a silly kiddish girl? Would you tell her to shut up? *Mah*ciah!'

And she started to dance about shouting the name. Billy was terribly embarrassed. What if Marcia came along? And Jake and Sharon remembered Mandy talking about Marcia before and wanted to know who she was, and why Billy ought to keep away from her.

'Marcia's his girlfriend,' Mandy said, and kept saying. Billy had to shout 'She's not!' and 'I haven't got one!' and 'She's not anybody!' when they kept going on at him.

Jake of course, the way he was feeling, had noticed that Mandy thought there was some connection between Marcia and drugs and he kept wanting to talk about that. He took no notice of what Mandy was saying now about girlfriends but just kept asking if Marcia was a pusher or anything. Sharon was interested in that too.

It was all a load of rubbish to Billy. Just because Mandy was a girl and had kiddish ideas about boyfriends and girlfriends, he was getting all this hassle from his friends and feeling like telling them to stuff themselves or jump in the river or something. He wasn't going to put up with it.

'You walk up Water Lane,' he shouted at Mandy. 'And count to a hundred at the top before you come back.'

Mandy stopped shouting and looked really shocked.

'No,' she said. 'That's not fair.'

But, to Billy's surprise, Jake and Sharon agreed with him.

'Go on,' they said.

Mandy walked away, staring back at them as if they'd done something terrible to her. 'Not fair,' she said two or three times while they could still hear her. She was walking very slowly. You could see she hoped they would change their minds.

'Thanks,' Billy muttered at the other two, and reeled in and cast again.

'*Is* she a pusher?' asked Jake. He wasn't going to drop it. He must have helped get rid of Mandy just so he could ask that again.

Billy sulked. He wished people would leave him alone. Jake and Sharon stared at him, waiting for his answer.

'She might be,' he mumbled. 'I don't know. How would I? I don't get stuff from her. I'm not thick.'

'I hope not,' said Jake.

'That glue was just a laugh,' said Billy. He could hear himself sounding as if he wasn't telling the truth, all because he knew they expected him to lie. They thought because he'd done it once he would probably do it again. It was like Jake had said about Josie – people just branded you. Dad had done it, Mandy was doing it, Jake was. Maybe now Sharon would start.

'Mandy's bothered about it,' Sharon said.

Billy said nothing.

'She's not stupid,' added Sharon.

'And I am, that's what you mean, isn't it?'

Sharon shook her head but Billy didn't believe her. 'Why can't you all shut up?' he shouted at them.

'All right,' said Jake, sitting down on the edge of the embankment. 'We'll just sit here, shall we, Sharon, quiet as little mice and not say boo 'cause Billy might get upset.'

Billy glared up Water Lane to see what Mandy was doing. She'd started all this.

She wasn't doing as she'd been told. She'd got as far as the gate to the warehouse and had stuck her hand through the wire mesh, pulling at something.

She stood up and started walking back. Billy shouted and waved again but she only started to run.

She panted over to them, holding whatever it was she'd pulled out of the warehouse yard so that no one else would see it.

'What're you doing here?' grumbled Billy. 'You're supposed to go right to the top, and count . . .'

'I've found something,' she said breathlessly, 'look.'

She showed them a small plastic packet like a tobacco pouch. In it was some stuff like dark brown Plasticine, a bit crumbly in places.

Billy thought of Marcia handing something under a table at the ice rink. He thought of her and Brian unloading boxes yesterday morning. They must have dropped this. The Colonel said they'd been in a hurry.

'Where'd you get that?' he asked, although he knew perfectly well.

'Just inside the gate,' said Mandy. 'What is it?'

Billy looked at Jake. 'D'you know, Jake?'

'Josie used to have that stuff.'

'Give's it here,' Billy took the pouch off Mandy. She yelled a bit until Sharon told her to hand it over.

Billy held it, wondering why he'd asked for it. He'd

88

thought it was better for him to have it than Mandy.

'What'll we do?' he asked Jake. 'Chuck it in the river?'

'We should take it to the police,' said Jake.

'Yes,' said Sharon.

'I'm not going to the coppers,' said Billy. 'They'll blame me for it.'

'Rubbish,' said Sharon. 'They treated you all right before. Took you home even. You weren't charged or anything. You were lucky.'

'Yeah,' said Billy. 'And they told me to stay out of trouble and they didn't want to see me again. If I turn up with this stuff they won't believe anything I say. You take it.' He held the bag at Jake.

Jake shook his head. 'Let's all go,' he said. 'The coppers aren't always very nice to us blacks. Especially with drugs in our possession. Josie says . . .' He stopped talking suddenly.

'I'll take it if you like,' said Sharon. 'Only Mandy'll have to come too, because she found it.'

And Billy would have to go with her, to keep an eye on her like he always promised. Anyway, it was feeble letting girls do something like this.

'What about the Colonel?' asked Mandy. 'He'd be all right, we could tell him and he could tell the police.'

'He's too old,' said Billy. 'Old people don't know anything about drugs. 'Cept the ones you buy in Boots'.'

They were standing there, holding the pouch where anyone could see it, when he saw Brian and Marcia come out of Water Lane and turn in their direction.

Billy snatched the pouch down by his side, then wished he hadn't. They might have seen Mandy at the warehouse gate and be suspicious. Marcia was saying something to Brian and he was shaking his head. She went on talking at him.

Jake and Sharon and Mandy looked to see what Billy was staring at. Brian and Marcia walked towards them.

Brian was smiling.

'Hello,' he said. 'You're our paper boy, aren't you?'

Billy nodded. The pouch clutched in his right hand felt as if it was two metres across.

'You're always early with it,' said Brian. 'We like that.'

'I have to be on time for school,' said Billy staring at the ground. He felt himself blushing. The others would laugh at him when this was over. He wanted to turn round and get on with his fishing. But he'd have to put the pouch down, and they'd grab it and take it away. He thought they shouldn't get it back.

'What's that you've got?'

Marcia was talking to him. It was the first time. He went all hot. Her voice made his toes tickle. But he didn't want to answer even if he could've breathed properly.

He looked around, the way he would in school if a teacher suddenly asked him that.

'That's my fishing rod,' he said. There it was, lying on the ground. He wasn't being cheeky, he was telling the truth.

'I mean that, in your hand,' said Marcia pointing. She started to sound like a teacher, or like a bossy adult anyway.

'What? Oh, *this*?' Billy held up the pouch and looked at it as if he was surprised to see it. The others were looking at him, wondering what he would do. Jake looked as if he might grab it and run if Billy went to hand it over. And he was looking at Marcia too, with a puzzled expression, as if he was trying to recognise her.

Sharon was looking up and down the tow path, probably hoping someone would come along who could help them. Mandy was staring at Marcia with wide-open eyes. She would go on about the shocking-pink jump suit later on, Billy could tell from her expression.

'Just something we found,' said Billy. He lowered the bag to his side again.

'I see,' she said. 'Where?'

Now she *was* talking like a teacher, as if she had the right to know every little thing about you when it suited her to ask.

'What's that to you?' asked Billy.

'You're a cheeky little brat, aren't you?' said Marcia. She was annoyed. You could find out a lot about adults by getting them angry.

'I'm not little,' said Billy, 'and I'm not cheeky either.'

'Oh yes you are,' said Marcia. 'Very cheeky.'

Any minute now she'd make a grab for the pouch. Billy tightened his grip on it.

'That was taken from private property,' said Marcia.

'Oh?' said Billy. 'Is it yours?'

Marcia nearly said 'Yes.' Then she changed her mind.

Brian butted in. 'No,' he said. 'But you've no right to have it.'

Behind Marcia's back, Sharon was pointing along the tow-path towards the bridge. She did it without moving her arm from her side, putting one finger out and moving her hand slightly. Billy saw the movement out of the corner of his eye. He looked at Marcia for a second or two longer, then moved his eyes sideways to see what Sharon had seen.

'Look out!' he said suddenly. 'Here comes a copper!' He watched Brian and Marcia jump. They looked at each other.

'I don't suppose it's anything important,' said Marcia.

'I thought it might be fish bait,' said Billy. 'I'll try it and see.'

'Do that,' said Brian. 'Best of luck.' He looked a bit sick.

'The fish might get hooked on it,' said Billy.

'Come on, Brian,' said Marcia. 'We're late.'

They walked away pretty quickly. Billy grinned. They looked back as they walked.

'Mandy,' said Billy, 'go and ask that copper what time it is.'

'Sharon's got her watch,' said Mandy.

'Do what I tell you. Quick. While they're looking.'

Mandy looked at Brian and Marcia. They were the other side of the slipway, looking back. She thought, smiled and did a big, slow, clumsy wink at Billy. She trotted off.

The copper had to bend down to hear what she was saying. She seemed to be pointing at Brian and Marcia, who turned and walked away.

Mandy came skipping back. 'Half-past eleven,' she said.

Billy watched the policeman walk to the bottom of Water Lane, stand still looking at the river and turn to go up the lane to the town. He could hand the bag over now, tell the story. Marcia and Brian would be caught. It would serve her right . . .

But he'd never pimped on anybody yet. Not even Martin. Not really. But *he* needn't do it. Sharon could. She'd said.

He looked at her. She was listening to Mandy explaining how she'd told the policeman they'd asked Brian and Marcia the time but had thought what they told them was wrong. That was how she'd been able to point at Brian and Marcia like that and scare them.

The policeman disappeared up the lane.

Sharon looked at the bag. 'It must be some sort of drug, mustn't it?'

'Yeah,' said Jake. 'It is. I know it is. And I'll tell you something else,' he added. 'I've seen Marcia before.'

Everyone was a bit surprised by that. By the way he said it.

'Along the tow-path?' Sharon didn't think that, you could tell. She was asking the question to make Jake say more.

'Nah. At a club in Putney. Couple of months ago. I was there 'cause Josie had a gig on the night I was going to see her. I remember, Marcia was wearing that jumpsuit.'

'I'd remember her anyway,' said Billy, then wished he hadn't.

'Do you think she's pretty, Sharon?' asked Mandy.

'Not pretty,' said Sharon. 'But you should ask Billy about that sort of thing. I wouldn't know.' She sounded really bitchy. Billy was surprised.

'When Josie'd done her first spot, she had a drink,' said Jake. 'And Marcia came and talked to her.'

'What about?' asked Sharon.

Chapter Eighteen

Jake was trying to remember. He could see, as he stared back into the past, a small, dark room with a lot of smoke in it. People sitting at little square tables, with drinks. The band, without Josie, playing on a little platform in the corner of the room, next to the steps which went up to the street. Everyone there older than himself, but no one really old.

There'd been an argument about him coming in. The guy on the door said he was too young, but Josie said he was with her and she was singing there that night. The guy said they would be risking their licence and Josie laughed at him.

Inside, another argument. Josie asked the waiter to bring Jake an orange juice, the waiter said they didn't do just orange juice, the kid'd have to have something in it. Josie swore at him, said she'd pay whatever it was for vodka and orange, if they were mean enough to charge their lead singer, but he could bring the orange juice without the vodka. 'Bring the bottle,' she'd added, to make sure. The waiter grumbled but brought a small bottle of orange and an empty glass. 'For the baby,' he'd said, and Josie had apologised to Jake.

He hadn't minded. He'd never been anywhere like that before and it was exciting.

When it was time, Josie went into another room at the side to change into another dress. Jake hardly recognised her when she came back in, took the microphone off its stand and held it up to her mouth as if she was going to eat it, like an ice cream or chocolate bar. The lights went all red, making Josie's dress and hair and skin shine. The dress was a lot of shiny bits like the scales on a fish. There was a gap like a capital V down the front of it that came to below her belly button. You could see the muscles in her stomach tighten and relax when she was singing. At the top, the dress hung loosely and you could see what was moving behind it. Not quite everything, but a lot more than Jake had seen of a real girl before. Josie had stopped being Josie. She was like someone in a film. Someone he didn't know, someone a bit frightening.

The first song she sang was fast and loud and Jake couldn't hear the words. The second one was slow and dreamy and she whispered it into the microphone as if there was no one else listening.

Take me and put me to sleep, Mr Sandman,
Drop your sweet dust in my eyes.
Show me the world that is hiding in this one,
Help me to realise
That the world is a game and you don't have to play it,
That the law is the same and I don't have to say it
Is right or it's wrong, 'cause it just doesn't matter,
Take me away,
Take me away.

Take me and take me apart, Mr Sandman,
Powder the blood in my veins.
Show me the world falling down, falling over,
Help me slip off the reins
That tie me to life in this God-awful city,
That blinker my eyes to the pain and the pity
Of living and working, of living and dying,
Take me away,
Take me away.

Jake came to himself suddenly. Sharon had him by one arm and Billy was holding the other. Mandy was in front of him, looking worried. 'Are you all right, Jake?' she was saying.

'You've gone pale,' said Billy, then laughed at what he'd said.

Jake sat down on the edge of the embankment and leaned his head forward. The others held on to him so he didn't fall in.

He sat up. 'A paler shade of black,' he said. Billy laughed

again. 'I'm all right,' Jake added. 'Just remembered something about Josie.' He hadn't thought of that song since the night he'd heard it, but now he remembered every word, the tune, the way Josie whispered into the microphone, the way the dress relaxed on her.

When she sat down next to him at the end of the spot, he told her he'd liked the song. 'That's good,' she said. 'I wrote it.'

Then Marcia, dressed in the same gear she had on today, had come and talked to Josie.

Jake looked up at the others. 'Marcia and Josie didn't say much to each other,' he said. 'They were fixing to meet each other the next day, somewhere. Marcia was going to give Josie something . . .'

'We can guess what that was,' said Sharon. Just for a minute she sounded exactly like her mother.

'Yeah,' he said. 'But it wasn't just for herself. I think Josie was going to pass some of it on to other people. I didn't know then, but she was a . . .'

It was a stinking rotten world. Josie was nice. She wouldn't have wanted to do those things. She must have been forced . . . He wished he could believe it. And he wished he could do something to hurt Marcia.

After Marcia had left the club, Josie'd done two more spots, changed her dress again, collected some money and taken Jake to the nearest bus stop. 'You'd better let them think you saw me at the flat,' she said. 'Otherwise they probably won't let you come again.' Jake had done that, because he knew she was right. So when his mum said his clothes stank of smoke he said there'd been people to dinner at the flat. And he said that when a man tried to give him a drink, Josie had been angry and insisted that he have only orange juice. So Mum, who'd been ready to say that if Josie was going to have all sorts there when Jake went it would be better if he didn't go, had been pleased and said Josie was a good girl at heart. And Jake still thought that was right, even now.

'It's time we went home for lunch, Billy,' said Mandy. 'We're not to be late, Mum said.'

'We've got a bit longer,' said Billy. He picked up the pouch again. 'What are we going to do with this?'

'You'd better make up your mind,' said Sharon. 'Those two are coming back again.'

Brian and Marcia were about a hundred metres away along the tow-path.

'We'd better get out of here.' Billy started dismantling his rod and chucking the bits into his bag all anyhow. Jake and the others did the same. Brian and Marcia seemed to quicken their pace. Billy shoved the pouch in amongst his fishing tackle and searched his pockets for the key to unchain his bike. Jake thought they could pretend they'd thrown the pouch in the river.

Then he heard a tapping sound behind them. The Colonel had come down the steps by the bridge and was walking over to them. He looked a bit surprised when they all rushed at him.

'Packing up?'

'My dad's going out this afternoon so we've got to be early for lunch,' said Mandy.

'Not all that early,' said Billy crossly. He never liked it if Mandy seemed to boss him around.

Brian and Marcia had stopped at the foot of the lane. Jake and the others walked past them with the Colonel. Even Mandy didn't look at them or say anything.

Jake thought they were all right as far as the Colonel's house. Then they'd have to move quickly. Billy could double Mandy. Jake and Sharon would just have to run.

They could hear music over what the Colonel was saying as they walked along. Mandy butted in to ask if he'd left his radio on. The Colonel snorted.

'I never listen to that sort of thing if I can help it,' he said. 'That din's from the fairground.'

'Is there a fair?' Billy beat the rest of them to asking the question, but not by much. 'Where?'

'The usual place,' said the Colonel. 'If you go through under the railway line you'll find it. In the field by the main road.'

'Are there dodgems?' asked Billy.

The Colonel wrinkled his moustache. 'I expect so. There are usually. Good bit of fun, dodgems.' He seemed to be remembering something from a long time ago.

'What's the time, Sharon?' Billy was looking in his pockets, pulling out money. 'We could have a go before lunch. It'll be 25p a car for us.'

'I've got to go,' said Sharon.

'Come on,' said Billy. 'If you go, there'll only be three of us. Someone'd have to ride by themselves and it'd cost more per person. Come on.'

The Colonel was looking from Billy to Sharon and back again, waiting to see who would get their way.

Sharon looked at her watch. 'All right,' she said. 'But just one ride.'

'Great!' shouted Billy. 'I've got 50p. Have you got anything, Jake?'

'Tell you what,' said the Colonel. 'Why don't I come with you and pay for your tickets?'

That put a really big grin on Billy's face. He even remembered to say 'Thank you.'

'My privilege, my dear chap,' said the Colonel. 'Let's toddle.'

As they toddled, Jake looked back to see what Brian and Marcia were doing. They were standing at the gate of their house and, as he looked, they went inside.

Chapter Nineteen

It took them a while to get to the fairground, going at the Colonel's pace, but Jake didn't think anyone would mind about that. He thought, in fact, that Billy made it a bit obvious how much he liked being given something, the way he chattered to the Colonel so much more than usual.

The dodgems were at the far end of the fairground from the entrance, past all the tombola stalls and the shooting galleries. Mandy wanted to look at the fish bowls and teddy bears that were prizes on those stalls, but Billy hurried her on.

The cars weren't moving when they arrived. One or two had people in them who had paid and were waiting to start. The man who ran them was shouting something you could hardly make out and jingling his flat leather bag of money.

Billy fixed his bike so that no one would take it. He took his fishing bag with him, checking that the zip was done right up. Jake and Sharon took theirs as well.

Billy tried to get Jake to go in the same car with him but Jake thought that would be boring because Billy would want to do most of the driving. 'Why not take Sharon?' he asked. Billy looked put out.

Sharon seemed to get bitchy again. 'Pity Marcia's not here,' she said to Billy. 'I suppose you'd let *her* go in a dodgem with you.'

Billy looked put out again at that, and the Colonel gave Jake a big wink. 'Wheels within wheels, eh?' he said. '*Cherchez la femme.*' Jake grinned at him, a bit surprised. It had never occurred to him before that Sharon might fancy Billy.

Then Billy got in a car and told Mandy to come with him. Sharon, getting in another alongside Jake, looked fed up. 'He just wants to do crazy things and thinks Mandy'll encourage him,' she muttered, glaring at Billy. Then she shut up.

Jake had an idea. 'If Mandy comes with me,' he said to Billy, 'and I keep my fishing bag and Sharon's, we'll both have about the same amount of room.'

Billy thought that was fair and told Mandy to get out. Sharon looked cross again. 'I'd sooner go with you,' she muttered at Jake.

'No you wouldn't,' he said, doing his biggest white teeth in black face grin. 'De white girls gotta go with de white boys, den all de folks be happy, baas.'

Sharon tried not to laugh. 'Isn't Mandy white?' she muttered at him.

'De tinies is different,' gibbered Jake. 'It's de *big* white girls got to go with white boys. Odderwise all de baad tings might happen, man.'

Sharon giggled and got out. 'Someone will think you mean that sort of thing one day and then where will you be?'

'Right where I is now, ma'am. Sitting in my place like a good little black boy, waiting for the white baas to hand out the goodies.'

The Colonel snorted and paid the man with the flat leather bag. Mandy jumped in beside Jake, and Sharon marched across to Billy. He was only interested in when the cars would start to move.

'Enjoy yourselves,' said the Colonel. 'I'll watch you start then toddle off' (he said 'orf') 'if you don't mind. I've one or two things to do.'

They were all saying 'Thank you' when the electricity was switched on.

For a minute all the cars seemed to be jammed against each other. Then one turned in a half-circle and shot out like a pip squeezed from an orange. It was like when you were shoving to get out of a classroom and someone had been stuck in the door.

Soon all the cars were moving. At first they all went in roughly the same direction and only banged into each other more or less by accident. Jake saw Billy leaning forward as if by doing that he could make his car go faster. Sharon was still looking a bit sour.

Mandy was sitting very still by Jake, holding herself back in her seat so that she wouldn't shoot forward and bang her face if they hit anything. She grinned at Jake when she saw him look at her. The Colonel was still at the edge of the platform, smiling vaguely. Jake wondered if he could see clearly enough to know which cars they were in. Then he waved his walking stick in the air and 'toddled orf'.

It was as if that was what people had been waiting for. Everyone started to crash each other. You looked ahead, saw another car pulling away from someone they had hit, not noticing you were coming straight at them. Bang. All your bones were shaken, your knees and elbows hit the wheel or the sides of the car. Mandy started to squeal and went on doing it. Jake saw her more than he heard her over the rumble of the dodgems and the shouting.

Suddenly they were driving straight at the end wall. Jake spun the wheel and they started to turn, then stopped still while the dodgem made up its mind which way it wanted to go next. Someone crashed into them behind. Mandy was thrown forward, then back again. She stopped squealing, looked at Jake, giggled and started to squeal again.

Billy shot past. Sharon had her hands on the wheel. Jake thought at first she was trying to make Billy drive sensibly, then he saw her deliberately ram another car broadside on. Her hair had come loose and she was laughing.

Jake shouted at Mandy to see if she wanted a go. She put her hands on the wheel and steered a bit, but they got hit three times while she was doing it and she gave the wheel back to Jake.

Jake decided to track down Billy and Sharon and ram them. He could see, through the criss-crossing cars, Billy's fair hair and Sharon's, which was longer than you thought when it came undone.

Jake dodged his way through until he was just behind Billy and Sharon. He waited his chance. Billy and Sharon were too busy passing the wheel back and forth to each other to notice anything else.

What happened next was all over very quickly but it stayed quite clearly in Jake's mind.

First, Billy's and Sharon's dodgem was hit from the other side and turned in front of Jake's. They saw him coming and shouted. He hit them. They were blocked by the car that had hit them first, which was up against the wall. All three stopped dead. Billy was shouting 'Get off,' at Jake and Mandy.

Then Jake saw a hand reaching around Billy, grabbing his fishing bag. In the middle of laughing he looked to see who it was. Marcia and Brian were in the car behind Billy.

Jake shouted at Billy to warn him and Billy noticed at the same time what was happening. He jumped around and grabbed the end of his bag. His dodgem started to move again as he and Marcia struggled.

Then Marcia let go of the bag with one hand, keeping a tight grip with the other. She slapped Billy's face very hard.

Billy shouted some swear-words and let go. His dodgem shot away and banged the rim of the platform. Billy, half-standing, fell over the side of the car and Sharon had to grab his hand to pull him back in. Jake's car moved slowly into the space where Billy's had been. Brian and Marcia had jumped out of theirs, on to the wooden rim and from there to the ground. They were running and Marcia was tearing at the zip of Billy's bag.

The dodgems stopped. From the far end, where the motor was operated, they saw the money-bag man and another one, coming towards them over the floor. They looked angry.

Billy and Sharon had hopped out of their car already. Billy ran to his bike, unlocked it, jumped on. Sharon helped Jake get Mandy down, then they all ran. You didn't stop to argue with fairground people, they knew that.

At the entrance they found Billy. He was picking up his bag, which had been dropped on the grass. Jake could see Brian and Marcia running down the street that led to the tow-path. He looked back to see if the dodgem men were coming, but they seemed to have given up.

'Did they break anything?' Sharon asked Billy.

He was looking carefully through his stuff. 'No,' he said. 'But they've got their stuff back.'

'Course,' said Jake.

Mandy was starting to look as if she might cry. Billy told her not to get upset. 'You're all right, so am I. We're coming back fishing this afternoon.'

'It won't be safe,' said Mandy.

'Nothing safer,' said Billy. 'They know what we know. We'll tell the police if they muck us about. I want to keep an eye on them and their warehouse.'

'That's right,' said Jake. 'I think we should.'

'Yes,' said Sharon.

'So you'll shut up at lunch-time,' said Billy to Mandy. 'We've been fishing all morning and the Colonel gave us a ride on the dodgems. That's all. Right?'

'All right,' said Mandy. She stopped looking weepy and grinned instead. 'It's fun, isn't it?'

Chapter Twenty

Brian put the phone down, moving like a man in deep shock.

'John,' he said to Marcia, who had just come in.

'What did he want?'

'Our blood, basically.' He stared out at the rain-stippled river as if at a high, blank wall.

'Go on,' said Marcia.

He shrugged. 'He's heard from Hugh where we've parked the stuff. He proposes to buy it from us, to take it off our hands, he says. For less than we paid for it. If we don't agree, he'll tip off the police. We are to deliver the goods, by boat, late on Sunday night.' He was talking flatly, as if he wasn't interested in what he was saying. 'He'll send a couple of heavies who'll make sure we do as he says. They'll blindfold us before we get anywhere near the drop point.'

Marcia nodded slowly. 'He's forcing us out.'

'Right. You won't deal in hard drugs. He thinks I'm not fit to deal in anything. So we're no use to him.'

Marcia picked up the phone and started to dial.

Brian took the receiver from her hand. 'No good,' he said. 'He's abandoned the office we knew. And his name's not John any more.'

Marcia felt herself beginning to shake and tried to laugh instead. 'You're making this up,' she said.

'I wish I was,' said Brian sadly. 'He's worked it all out. Next Monday we shall be ordinary members of the Thamesford Traders' Association.'

Marcia shook her head. 'If it really comes to that,' she said, 'I won't be staying with you.'

Brian turned away. 'You bitch,' he said.

Chapter Twenty-One

Late on Sunday afternoon Billy and the rest were just packing up fishing when they saw a van pull up at the warehouse in Water Lane. Marcia and Brian got out and opened the gates and the back of the van.

'What are they doing?' asked Mandy.

'We've got to find out,' said Billy.

Jake looked up the lane, thought a bit and said, 'I'll go. They won't recognise me.'

'Course they will,' said Billy. 'You were with us yesterday.'

'All West Indians look the same, don't you know that? Anyway, I'll sneak up on them . . . Can I have your bike?'

Billy never let anyone borrow his bike. But he knew it would be stupid to argue with Jake now. He took the key from his pocket and released his bike from the railings.

'I'll go up the steps by the bridge, round the block and down the lane from the top,' said Jake, taking it.

'Good idea,' said Sharon. 'They won't think you're anything to do with us at all. We'll stay here where they can see us.'

'Yeah,' said Billy. Mandy was looking at Jake as if he was going to do something very exciting and dangerous.

'At the gate,' said Jake, looking at Billy, 'I'll fall off and have a good look in while I'm picking myself up.'

'No you won't,' said Billy, stepping forward and grabbing at the handle bars. But Jake saw him coming and got away. He hopped on and circled round Billy, who didn't want to rush him in case he fell off and scratched the paint. Worse still, he might go over the edge into the river.

'There's no need to fall off. If you do that' – Billy searched around for some reason other than the real one, that he didn't want his bike damaged – 'they'll notice you for sure.'

Jake stopped the bike. 'Smart,' he said, nodding. 'I'll have to think of something else. You see, if I bike straight past I won't have time to see anything. See ya!' And he jumped on and rode to the steps.

It seemed a terribly long time to Billy before they saw Jake again at the top of the lane. When they did see him, what he was doing worried Billy a bit, but not as much as falling off would have done. It was a clever idea, Billy had to agree.

Jake was riding backwards and forwards across the lane, jumping the front wheel on to the footpath on each side and doing a very tight turn. The gutters weren't deep, so he wouldn't damage the wheels. It took him ages to get as far as the parked van.

He carried on that way until a car coming down the lane tooted at him. Then he rode fast down the middle of the road and pulled up by them, jamming the brakes on and skidding around in a big circle.

Billy didn't say anything until Jake was safely off the bike and had given it back.

Then, 'What'd you see?' he asked.

Mandy was telling Jake he was clever to ride like that and Billy told her to shut up because he could see Jake would show off about it before he told them anything.

'They're loading cardboard boxes into the van,' Jake said at last. 'Brian's up in the doorway at the top of that belt thing, handing them down to Marcia. I don't think they noticed me, they were too busy. And,' he said, eyes and teeth flashing, 'Brian was saying they'd load the boat at ten.'

'Billy,' said Mandy, 'it's time we were going home.'

'Yeah,' said Billy. He was taking his rod to pieces and putting the bits into his bag. 'Go along to the bridge and I'll catch you up.'

She wandered off. Billy waited until she couldn't hear him and said, 'Jake, could you get back here tonight?'

Jake looked doubtful. 'What would I tell Mum and Dad? They always want to know where I am. They'll be at church. I could sneak out, but . . .'

Sharon said, 'Why don't you go to church with them? There's a youth social after the service tonight. You can say you'll stay. I will too. Then we can get away and come down here.'

Billy and Jake gazed at Sharon with open mouths. Then Jake grinned, a big, devilish grin. 'You wicked, sinful girl,' he said, 'inviting a boy to a social so you can sneak off with him.' He winked at Billy. 'She fancies me, this one.' He put his arm round her shoulders.

She waited a minute then shrugged him off. 'I couldn't fancy *you*,' she said, opening her eyes very wide and looking up at him, 'not someone who can ride a bike that slowly without falling off. I mean, I can see such a person is far too clever for *me*.'

'Get off,' said Jake.

'I want to know what's going on as much as you do, that's all,' she added. 'All right?'

'Great,' said Jake.

'My Gran's coming to dinner,' said Billy, 'I'll have to be there. They'll talk for ages. But they'll go down the pub afterwards, they always do. So I'll sneak out when they've gone and Mandy's asleep. I'll leave my pillow humped to look as if I'm there. I did it once before.'

Sharon looked a bit unhappy about that. 'You shouldn't.'

'How's it different from what you're doing?' asked Billy.

She looked more unhappy. Billy grinned at her. He didn't want her to think he was getting at her. She might change her mind.

'You'd better go,' she said. 'Mandy's coming back to fetch you. See you tonight.'

Chapter Twenty-Two

The Colonel reached across the small table and switched off the radio. The news had just ended. The world was as crazy as ever. Sometimes he was glad he wouldn't have to be part of it much longer. Not, usually, in the mornings when he went out for his first breath of fresh air and a look at the garden. That always made a good start to the day, rain or shine. But when he came back in and remembered, as he had every day for ten years, that there was no point in taking a cup of tea up to the bedroom because Maisie was no longer there to drink it, he felt the awful emptiness of the days left to him stretching away like interstellar space. And when, by an effort of will, he tried to interest himself in the world through which he moved like a stranger, he found it full of pointless, random violence and death, of vicious behaviour of all sorts.

So he would potter out along the tow-path, talking to anyone who would pass the time of day with him; children Brian and Marcia, strangers. A few words and then on, before they let the boredom show in their faces, while they were still thinking nice old boy, never gives any trouble.

He'd never been ill, thank God, and he could do the little bit of cooking and washing, fatigue duties to keep himself smartly on parade a few years longer. He hoped that when his time came it would be sudden and quickly over. There would be no one left behind for whom the shock would be very great. Just a lot of vague acquaintances who'd happen not to see him about anymore.

On Sunday evenings he would wash up after his tea – a slice or two of toast and gentleman's relish and a few cakes from the pastry shop in the town – and trot off to the Coach and Horses for a snort or two to keep out the cold. People sometimes talked to him there, and even if they didn't it was company of a sort. You overheard conversations about ordinary concerns, kept in touch that way.

He dried his few crocks and put them on the table in the kitchen ready for breakfast. Methodical habits had once helped him save time. Now they helped him fill it. By always being ready for what was coming next, whether it be breakfast, next season's flowers and vegetables, or a reunion in London, he always had a sense of something needing to be done before the uselessness of his continued existence could be pushed aside no longer.

He took his stick from the hallstand and tossed up whether to take his tweed overcoat. It would be the first time since April if he did, an admission that winter was on the way; but it had been very fresh that afternoon. Nothing worse than to get home cold again after a warm evening.

He put the stick back on the stand and reached down the coat, got himself into it. The simplest thing took so long.

Coat on, stick in hand, he checked the back door then walked through to the front, putting out lights as he went. They said you should leave one to frighten off burglars. He never did. He'd grown up in a world where burglars only entered houses where they expected to find something valuable, which couldn't apply to his. He knew that nowadays young louts would break in and smash places up just for the fun of the thing, out of some sort of envy it was supposed to be. Well, if they were silly enough to envy him . . .

He was glad he wasn't a youngster now. No jobs, no army to speak of, nothing to do unless you were lucky. And the ways and means of messing your life up increasing every day. Drugs, sex, vandalism.

It was cold outside. A wind coming down the river that got in at every unprotected spot. His defences were not what they had been. He weighed much what he always had, that was true, but on cold nights he felt thinner.

There was a light in the front room next door. Brian sitting at his desk working through some figures. No sign of Marcia. In Water Lane he noticed that the gates of the warehouse were padlocked and there was no sign of the van he'd seen them loading that afternoon.

The pub he used was in another of the town's narrow alleys. There'd been several different landlords behind its bar since he'd been going there, but they hadn't really changed the place from what it had been. There was a television set now, certainly, and one of those noisy coin-in-the-slot gramophones. There were some one-armed bandits as well, as they called them, but they were at the back near the latrines and didn't trouble him much.

He was given his usual pint of black-and-tan straight away and exchanged small talk with the landlord until someone else needed serving. He watched a darts match. Most of the players were regulars and called some greeting to him.

After a while there was a vacant table near the fire and he sat down. He eased his coat off. The television was on, but it was showing snooker and the commentary was quiet. The fire warmed his feet.

Collecting empty glasses, the landlord took his and brought him his second drink. 'One for yourself, George?' George had an orange juice and brought the change. Half-a-dozen chaps come to look at an interesting bit of the snooker, standing between him and the set. One of them apologised for blocking his view.

'Don't trouble yourself,' said the Colonel. 'I'm a cricket and rugger man myself.'

'Cheers.'

Two men in black jackets with leather patches came in and ordered double whiskies. They were looking for a seat by the fire, he could see that. He moved his feet and stick to let them know he didn't mind them joining him.

'Thanks mate. Cold out.'

The Colonel said 'Yes,' but didn't try to keep the conversation going. Try as he might, he couldn't accustom himself to being called 'mate'.

One of them swallowed half of his whisky and said to the other, 'We'd better not be too long.'

His companion looked at his watch. 'Nothing's happening until ten. That's well over an hour. Jim'll keep an eye out. We should've thought to bring a flask too. He knows how to look after himself.'

'Never worked with him before.'

'He knows what it's about.'

'He won't tell the guvnor we've left him?'

'No. What a job.' He finished his drink. 'Cold as an Eskimo's nose. Hanging about. I don't know why I bother.'

'The money's good.'

'Yeah. Same again?'

He stood up, looked at the Colonel.

'Can I get you something, mate?'

The Colonel pointed to his half-full glass. 'I'm all right, thanks.'

'Get you one of these to help it down.' He waved the two whisky glasses.

'That's uncommonly civil of you!' Never look a gift horse in the mouth. The chap was grateful to be allowed a place by the fire.

'Cheers,' they all said when he returned. The Colonel sipped his whisky and closed his eyes. He sometimes dropped off for a minute or two.

'When did the guvnor ring you?'

'Last night. Late. Rush job.'

'Same here. When do you think we'll be finished?'

'Not late. Ten o'clock they get their boat going. We get on board opposite the lock, blindfold them. They think they're going to the East End. They must be soft. Won't give any trouble.'

'You'd better be careful . . .'

The Colonel slightly opened one eye. The second man was pointing at him. 'He's asleep. He won't wake up again until they throw him out.'

He was half-inclined to sit up and demand an apology. But

what he was hearing was more interesting than that would be.
He gave a little snore, very quiet. It seemed to go down well.
They went on talking.

'How far to where we unload?'

'Ten minutes, quarter of an hour. We unload, then take
them well down river to confuse them. Then we can go
home.'

'Why didn't he send a lorry?'

'You've seen the place. It's cramped and it's public. Anyone
happens along and you're in dead trouble. This way, they have
the risk and hassle of getting it out of there. I think the guvnor
wants them to suffer a bit. The way he was talking they'd got
up his nose somehow.'

'Better go now.'

The Colonel heard them standing up, then felt a hand
shaking his shoulder.

'Night, mate.'

'I say,' said the Colonel, exaggerating his accent to amuse
them, 'I must have dropped orf. Thanks awfully. Good
night.'

They went out, grinning at each other.

Well now, what to do? He could imagine the desk sergeant if
he went into the station and started pitching this yarn. 'I see,
sir, you were sitting in a pub, having a quiet one or two, when
some criminal types sat next to you and plotted to move
something unknown from one place, unknown, to another,
unknown, by boat? Now, sir, why would they talk like this in
your hearing? They thought you were asleep. Well sir,
perhaps you'll forgive the question, but are you absolutely
sure you weren't? No offence sir, but I expect you do sometimes drop off of an evening. Especially when you've had a
quiet one or two. Just what had you had to drink, may I ask?
Two pints and a small whisky? Not a lot if you're used to it,
sir, I agree, but enough to make anyone less than totally
clear-headed. Tell you what, sir, we'll just ask a man to walk
home with you, and if there's any funny business going on

down at the river, sir, I expect he'll notice it. If not, well, no harm done . . .'

Whatever was going on, if anything was, it was not his concern. They weren't Russian spies. They weren't planning a murder. Thieves, perhaps. And if it was anything to do with Brian and Marcia . . . That worried him a little. He felt some loyalty to them as neighbours if not quite as friends. But . . .

At this point he must actually have nodded off for a time.

He came to with a slight start. There was certainly a whisky glass, not quite empty, in front of him. Two others. His pint, which he now finished. Perhaps George would know the two men.

Best thing would be to trot off home. He could keep a weather eye. Anything definitely suspicious he could report to the police.

He finished the whisky, in no great hurry. He said good-night to George and a few other familiar faces, got himself buttoned up against the wind and went out.

The High Street was quiet. Later, gangs of youths who had nothing better to do would come and shout in it.

Water Lane was deserted. He walked down carefully, not wanting to slip on the cobbles. He looked at his watch under a street lamp. Quarter-past ten. Whatever was happening should be under way.

There was a sudden burst of shouting somewhere ahead of him. He stopped. He didn't want to walk into trouble.

A small figure appeared around the corner of the lane, running towards him, shouting. It was followed by a second and a third. He turned, wanting to be nearer the safety and lights of the High Street. The small figure caught up with him.

'Colonel, Colonel, help!'

It was Mandy.

'Colonel,' she repeated, grabbing at his sleeve. 'Get the police. Billy's on that boat over there and they're kidnapping him.'

Chapter Twenty-Three

Billy thought his mum and dad would never get around to taking his gran off to the pub. And when they'd gone, Mandy almost seemed to suspect something and wouldn't go to bed for ages.

It was nearly nine o'clock when he thought it was safe to go. The dishes which he'd said he'd see to were all done and Mandy was asleep. He fixed his own bed so that anyone glancing in would be fooled, shut his door, left the landing light on and sneaked downstairs and out of the house.

It didn't take long to get to Thamesford. Apart from it being dark, it was so like coming to fish that he nearly jumped on his bike as the foot of the steps to ride to the slipway as usual.

But he thought he'd better be careful and it was then that the strangeness of what he was doing struck him. He began to feel nervous.

He took his bike under the arch of the bridge to be out of sight while he looked around.

The tow-path was empty. The fancy lights which they had in this bit of the town centre were quite a way apart but you could be pretty certain there was no one there. There were a lot of shadows in the doorways of boatsheds and other buildings. The one or two lawns that stretched down to the tow-path, with trees and bushes rustling, were creepy. Billy had never really thought about the place before but now it seemed a long way from the bridge to the slipway and what he saw looked unfriendly. Things he'd never noticed in daylight – creaking gates, tumbledown bits of fence – might have danger hiding in them.

Had Jake and Sharon come? They mightn't have been able to get away from that church thing. If they weren't around he was by himself in the dark and he didn't know what was going to happen.

If Brian and Marcia saw him there'd be trouble. They'd know he was there to spy on them.

There were some tall weeds between the path and the railings above the river. He pushed the bike in behind them, making a terrific rustling noise. When it was more or less out of sight to anyone who wasn't actually looking for it, he stood quite still and listened. The river hissed. A bus went over the bridge above his head.

He walked out of the archway on to the unshadowed tow-path. Far from being dark, it seemed as bright as day. The river gleamed and the cloudy sky had far more light in it than you could explain, seeing there was no moon. The tow-path had a pool of light on it every twenty or thirty metres under the lamps. On the bridge behind him and amongst the streets on the other side of the river behind the row of boats and the island, there was a yellowy-orange glow. Walking on the whitey-grey concrete squares, Billy felt like a fly crawling across the breakfast table with Dad's hand swooping down from in front to catch it. 'They can't see straight ahead, Billy, that's where you have to be to catch them.' Billy could see straight ahead, but that was his only advantage over the fly.

He ran to the foot of the steps and crouched to look again along towards the slipway without being seen himself. Nothing. He stood up and pushed around the corner of the boatsheds, back to the wall and hands spread to feel his way.

The boatsheds were painted white. He might as well have been in the beam of a searchlight. Anyone who saw him would know he was up to mischief.

He forced himself to walk normally, but stepped into the concealing darkness of the first boatshed doorway, and listened and looked. Nothing, except the hiss of the river and the sounds of air in his nose and throat. A gust of wind set something knocking in the shed behind him, quickly at first, then more slowly. The trees on the island all rustled together

114

like someone turning over in bed. Because the wind kept blowing, the trees kept on with their noise.

He ran to the next patch of shadow. Never mind if anyone saw him. And to the next. Four more and he was by the buildings on the corner of Water Lane.

The ramp was just a few metres from him. The boats across the river were in line, rocking gently as the wind nudged at them. He had lost all idea of what time it was and how long he had been there. It looked as if nothing was going to happen.

The wind dropped and everything went quiet. Then he heard something driving down Water Lane. A van. He knew who that had to be.

He couldn't stay where he was. There was nothing to hide him except the narrow shadow in a doorway. They would be only a few metres away. They must see him. He couldn't run back the way he had come – there were too many gaps between the shadows.

Two metres in front of him was the tree in the tub with the seat around it. The concrete was white and spooky-looking in this light.

Down on his hands and knees, he scooted across the gap and hid under one of the seats. It was wet and there were dead leaves and maybe a lot of other horrible things under there. He thought of spiders, then thought he'd better not think of them.

The van arrived at the ramp. He heard Brian say, 'You take the dinghy.' He tried to hold himself so that his clothes wouldn't get too dirty. Mum would go spare if they did.

Feet crunched the gravel in the slipway. Something splashed. A quiet noise of oars.

Lying very still, turning his eyes across the width of the tow-path that stretched away from his nose, Billy saw Marcia row across to their motor boat and climb aboard. She looked across the river, almost as if she could see Billy, waved.

She went down into the cabin. The engine started, not so loudly as Billy had expected. Just a mutter which didn't add much to the noises of wind and another bus on the bridge and Billy's heart thumping. The boat pulled out of line and its

115

headlamp came on. Billy hid deeper under the seat. A bit of crunching and slapping as the boat nosed into the ramp. Brian's feet on the gravel. Then, ten stiff, uncomfortable minutes while they moved boxes from van to boat and Billy wondered what to do.

And the sound of small feet running somewhere between here and the bridge, and Mandy's voice shouting, 'Billy! Billy!'

Chapter Twenty-Four

Billy was on his feet shouting at Mandy to go away. Brian and Marcia were shouting at each other. And a man came out of Water Lane, a tall black shape with a face white on top of it.

Mandy ran at Billy and grabbed him. The man rushed at both of them. Billy kicked his shins and the man swore.

The boat revved up loudly then cut out. Marcia swore as well. Again the man came at Billy, who had grabbed Mandy's wrist and was pushing her away behind him. A huge hand seized his shoulder. Billy let go of Mandy and shouted at her to run, twisting in the man's grip and letting fly with kicks that didn't hit anything.

The man, dodging Billy's feet, overbalanced and fell. Billy jumped up on to the seat. Mandy stood at the foot of Water Lane, shouting. The man got up and looked around for Billy.

In the slipway the boat coughed and spluttered as Marcia tried to restart it.

The man stood still, looking at Billy. He wasn't going to rush him, Billy could see that. Instead, he was calling to Brian. 'Come up here and we'll get this brat.' Mandy had stopped shouting and was coming towards them again. Billy yelled at her to get away. Whatever happened to him, she'd got to get out of this and be all right.

Brian came up the slipway around the van. He walked towards Billy from behind as the other man closed on him from in front. The boat engine fired and roared. Marcia shouted something.

Billy backed around the curve of the seat. There was nowhere to go but the river. And the boat, which was running smoothly now.

He jumped off the seat and ran to the jutting corner of the

117

slipway. The boat was below him, Marcia standing in it looking up. He jumped straight at her.

There was a tangle of arms and legs and she was shouting in his ear.

Billy got free and stood up. He had fallen off Marcia, down the steps into the cabin. She lay across them between him and the deck. His back was against the cardboard boxes. The motor cut out again.

Marcia was trying to get up. Billy's hands scrabbled at the top box, trying to prise it free. As he got hold of it she came down the steps towards him. He tried to throw it at her but it was too heavy for him to make a proper job of that. It hit her in the chest, and she fell back on the steps, gasping for breath. The boat started drifting out into the river.

Marcia stood up. There was nothing Billy could do except wait to be caught.

He made another desperate dive at the box, but when he tried to pick it up it came apart at the joints. Plastic pouches spilled everywhere.

He grabbed a handful and threw them in Marcia's face. He threw some more over the side. He threw them in the air like sweets at a birthday party. He stuffed a couple in his pockets. They would never get away with this. The bags would be drifting in the river. The police must find them.

Marcia brushed past him and went into the cabin. The motor started again and the boat swung towards the shore. Brian and the other man were waiting for him.

Billy scrambled over the cabin roof to the front of the boat. He got in front of the window through which Marcia was trying to steer. The boat hit the side of the slipway and lurched. Billy had just time to jump across, grabbing the railings as the boat fell away under his feet.

He heard Brian shouting, 'Get the boat clear. I'll get the kid,' as he scrambled through the rails. He ran, in the only direction he could, along the tow-path towards Brian's house, and the Colonel's.

There were no lights in the Colonel's house or he would

have knocked. He looked into the alley that would take him back into the centre of town. Someone was coming through it, a short man Billy didn't know, passing through a pool of light.

Billy feared this might be another of them and ran on. Brian was coming along behind him, horribly fast.

The lock bridge was on his left now, its pretty, old-fashioned lights showing up the fancy iron work and the big floodgates which hung above the water ready to be lowered when the tide came in.

The lock keeper's house was all dark as Billy ran up the steps on to the narrow bridge. Brian was not far behind him.

Billy was starting to get a stitch because he wasn't used to all that running, but he tried to put on speed. If he could get across, down the steps on the other side and into one of the little streets there, he might still be all right.

But it was useless. A man dressed in black was standing at the far end of the bridge, smoking. When he saw Billy coming he moved into the middle of the path, blocking Billy's way.

Brian called, 'Stop that boy, he's a thief,' and the man said, 'Right, squire.'

Billy stopped.

He was by one of the pillars of the bridge. There were iron cross pieces on a lower level between it and another pillar on the upstream side of the floodgates. Billy climbed on to the railing of the footway and jumped down onto one of them. He landed easily, without overbalancing, and walked along it until he got to the other pillar. He turned and faced Brian, who was shouting at him that he was a fool.

The man walked across to Brian. 'The boat should be here by now,' he grumbled.

Brian pointed angrily at Billy. 'He interfered and made a mess. Stuff all over the place. We can't leave it. The boat'll be here soon. Meantime we've got to catch this kid and take him with us.'

Billy thought there was no way he would let that happen.

The two men looked across at him.

'Come off there, kid,' said the man.

'No,' said Billy.

'We'll come and get you.'

'Come on, then.'

Billy looked at where he was standing. The iron was about twenty centimetres wide and there were three bits that width quite close together. Brian or the man could come and get him quite easily if they wanted. But if he got down on to the floodgates themselves, that would be different. There was the long straight top of the gate and a curved iron piece like a bow window in front of it. Below, a long way down, he could see the river.

He didn't want to think about that. Instead, he climbed slowly and carefully down. The man turned away from Brian who was shouting again. The best thing, Billy decided, was to sit on top of the gate and ease himself along it holding on with both hands. He reached the middle and stopped.

'I'm telling you, kid, come off there,' said Brian.

Billy didn't even bother to reply. Behind him he heard the boat revving up. He sneaked a look around and saw it pulling away from the bank and downriver. It wouldn't take long to get to the bridge. Then it would have to stop while they caught him, or leave him behind.

'What do we do?' It was Brian asking.

'Your problem, squire. If we don't catch him, there's no way Jim and I will be getting on your boat. We've been told to disappear if anything awkward happens. We always obey orders.'

Brian scrambled over the railings. 'Come off there, kid. You'll only get hurt.' He wasn't bossing now, he was begging. Once again Billy said nothing.

Brian walked along the iron crosspiece. He made a tall black silhouette against the sky. He was only a few metres away from Billy. He didn't look very steady.

In the lock keeper's house a telephone started to ring. The man on the path said, 'That's it, squire, I'm off,' and ran along the path to where he'd come from, down the steps and away.

120

The boat engine got louder. Lights came on in the house and the telephone stopped ringing.

Brian looked upstream at the boat. It was half-way towards them. He glared down at Billy, then edged his way back to the path and ran away in the same direction as the man.

The door of the lock keeper's house opened and someone ran out in pyjamas. He disappeared.

There was a humming sound. The gate under Billy jerked, and began to move down towards the water.

Billy thought all he had to do was hang on. The tide wasn't high so the gate would be well above the surface, he reckoned. But he wasn't absolutely sure. He hung on so tight his hands hurt.

The bottom of the gate hit the water, which boiled around it, frothing and bubbling as it forced its way back up from under the gate, making a sound like one of those big waterfalls in Africa or America where millions of gallons tumble over the edge of a high plateau.

His knuckles ached and water splashed his feet.

People were running along the tow-path. Some of them were police. The lock keeper had appeared again and was looking at Billy.

The engine of the boat, which had become very loud, cut out. There was a terrific flash of light and a bang as if a bomb had gone off, then clouds of thick, funny-smelling smoke were around Billy, choking him.

A hand appeared on the gate just along from Billy and someone pulled themselves out of the water to sit on the gate next to him.

It was Marcia.

Chapter Twenty-Five

Marcia waited for them to come and get her. They did, in time, but showed her her proper place by fetching the wretched boy first. The copper who finally walked along the top of the floodgate to help her balance her way back to dry land was obviously trying, not very hard, not to laugh. She felt like a performing seal being clumsily hauled out of its tank. Her black trousers and shirt clung clammily and her hair, straightened to its full length, moulded itself over her ears and neck.

In the lock keeper's garden where policemen and children were milling about, where the Colonel stood tall and distant in the background, Marcia noticed sulkily that there was no sign of Brian. No doubt he had applied his own convenient logic and run for it. 'No point in both of us getting caught if we can avoid it, you must see that . . .' She saw it all right.

Every so often the wind would send a cloud of cannabis smoke eddying through the garden. Thinking to reduce the bulk of the evidence against them by igniting the spare can of petrol, she hadn't reckoned with the pungent odours that would be released. She'd been lucky, too, not to be burnt in the explosion. Some policemen had got buckets and a fire-extinguisher from the lock keeper and were trying to douse the blaze.

The policeman who seemed to be in charge answered a crackle from his walkie-talkie, seemed pleased, talked to his colleagues and looked up at the bridge. A couple of others appeared up there, escorting a third figure who turned out, rather to Marcia's satisfaction, to be Brian.

The Colonel spoke to the officer in charge, then came to Marcia. 'Are you all right, young lady?' he asked.

She nodded. Water ran down her back.

'You'll be able to get in touch with your lawyer from the station, they assure me. You have got one, I expect?'

'Yes.'

'I must say I'm sorry. Not that you got caught, but that you needed to be.'

'Thank you,' said Marcia. It was a sort of compliment. She would accept it as one.

The Colonel turned away. Several children gathered around him.

The fair-haired paper boy wasn't one of them and Marcia looked vaguely around. She saw him soon enough, talking excitedly to a policeman, pulling one of the incriminating packets from his trouser pockets. She and Brian had brought pleasure and excitement into someone's life, if not quite in the way they had intended.

She ought to hate the kid for what he'd done to them. Months of hassle to come, all the fancy dress nonsense of a trial, jail for however long some pompous old fool of a judge took it into his head to give them, the shop probably lost, the house as well, maybe. All because of a cheeky little brat poking his nose into other people's business. That and the stuffy ideas of a tired old society run by tired old people who passed tired old laws.

She was working herself up into a tremendous rage at the injustice of it all when she remembered what she'd always said to Brian about hard drugs. He'd had his plans for her and such as the paper boy quite clear in his head. Start them smoking grass, move them on, to pills, mainline. Take their money, don't get caught. To hell with them.

She would tell the police all she knew about Brian, about John. When she and Brian were walked along the tow-path to a van, Brian ignored her and she him. They had nothing going for them now. The game they had played was over and they had lost.

Chapter Twenty-Six

Mandy had never been inside a police station before and she would have been frightened if the Colonel hadn't come with them. He'd suggested to the police that they interview the children at his house, but they'd apologised and said they couldn't do that.

At the station, a doctor looked at Billy to make sure he was all right and a nice lady policeman asked Mandy some questions and she'd told her how she'd found Billy wasn't in his bed and she knew where he must have gone so she followed him. Later she heard Sharon and Jake explaining how they'd come down Water Lane just in time to see Mandy run to the Colonel and the Colonel going to a phone box to call the police.

The Colonel rang all their parents – the police said he could do that if he really wanted to do something – to explain. Mandy'd heard him telling her mum and dad that Billy was a brave and public-spirited lad. She hoped they wouldn't be mad at Billy again. It wasn't his fault this time.

Now they were all in a sort of waiting room like at a doctor's. A policeman had gone down to the river to fetch Billy's bike. Their mums and dads would be along soon to fetch them home and they'd all been given cups of tea. The Colonel was sitting there smiling the way he had when Mandy had been drying out in front of his fire (here there was a big electric fire with both bars on). Billy was telling them about throwing drugs all over the place and Sharon and Jake were explaining how they hadn't been able to get away from the social and that was why they were late. No one was really listening.

A door in the corner opened and two policewomen came out with Marcia between them. They'd got her some dry clothes and she'd combed her hair a bit, but the way she looked now, Mandy reckoned, Billy wouldn't think she was half so smashing as he had.

In fact he took almost no notice. He was what their mum called 'full of himself', telling Sharon about jumping on to the floodgates and balancing there ten metres above the water.

It was Jake who took notice. He got up and walked over so he was standing in front of Marcia. The policewomen asked him to move out of the way.

Jake just looked at Marcia. 'You killed my aunty,' he said, and spat on the floor in front of her. Then he burst into tears.

Chapter Twenty-Seven

In John's other flat, the one Brian and Marcia knew nothing about, the one where he was known as Mr Wilberforce, he was talking briskly into the phone. Bill had rung after getting away from the shambles at Thamesford.

'I see,' he said. 'The nub is that the coppers have got them.'

He listened a moment longer, said good bye and hung up. This was not what he had wanted. He'd got the tides right, he'd got everything right except for a gang of interfering kids. He should have gained a load of cannabis more or less without cost to himself and got shot of Brian and Marcia as well. Instead there'd be a lot of hassle. He might even have to disappear.

He made a series of phone calls.

Chapter Twenty-Eight

Billy fell asleep with a big grin on his face. His dad had wanted to get mad at what he'd done, sneaking out like that, and running Mandy into danger, but the police and Mum and the Colonel hadn't let him. Then Dad changed his mind and said he was proud of Billy.

For once in his life he'd done something that everybody liked. It might never happen again.

They'd promised to take him and Mandy skating again on Thursday. This time, with Marcia out of the way, he'd concentrate properly. Mum had said maybe she could take them to lessons in the afternoon after school.

The Colonel had said he was a good lad.

He closed his eyes and dreamed of catching the biggest fish in the world. When he pulled it out of the water he found Martin stuck up to his waist in its mouth.